CONQUERING THE HEART OF THE BAD BOY

KNOX BROTHER OF ARBOR SHORES BOOK THREE

NOMI SUMMERS

Write from the Heart Books
P.O. Box 66202
St. Pete Beach, FL 33736

Cover Design by Elizabeth Mackey Designs

ISBN-13: 978-1-7332773-4-1

CHAPTER 1

*E*mma Woods rolled over in her bed, only to be greeted by a warm, wet tongue on the side of her face. She recognized this all too familiar morning routine well and knew that meant it was time to get up.

"No need for an alarm clock with you around, Zeke," she told the large black Lab who was standing at her bedside, chin resting on her mattress, sad puppy dog eyes looking up at her, pleading for his breakfast.

She scratched the top of Zeke's head and glanced at the clock on her nightstand: 6 a.m. Just like clockwork. She would swear this dog could tell time. She was convinced he was the smartest dog on earth, and she loved him for it. He was her protector, her confidante—her everything. She got Zeke nine years ago as a puppy, and it had been just the two of them in this great big house ever since.

Zeke made her feel safe, not that there was any cause for concern on Main Street in the heart of Arbor Shores. This small town was as safe as they came; the kind of town where you never lock your doors and you sleep with the windows open. Just as she had last night, and now the cool morning breeze was sweeping through the open window of her master suite. Sheer, white, floor-length curtains blew wildly as a gust of wind moved through the room. She sat up, closed her eyes, and took in a deep, invigorating breath. It was nearing the end of an Indian summer, and mornings were getting cooler again, just how she liked them.

Emma shuffled out of bed and straight to the shower. She got dressed and ready for the day ahead before making her way to the long staircase of her historic home. She ran her hand down the wood railing of the staircase as she descended and made a mental note that it needed to be sanded down before she ended up with a splinter. It sure could use a fresh coat of stain as well. Time was taking its toll on the old house, and it wasn't quite the beauty it once had been when her parents owned it. Growing up here, it was a focal point of the town; the tallest white Victorian on Main Street. Up until their deaths, her parents had run a bed and breakfast out of it.

She remembered always having travelers in and out all summer long when the tourists flocked to Arbor Shores to take in all that the quaint, coastal Northern Michigan town had to offer. Each year, many of the same families returned, and she'd come to know them as her own extended family. But those times seemed so long ago; nobody had stayed in the guest rooms in years.

As she made her way into the kitchen—the same kitchen where her mother would prepare breakfast and fresh bread each day for their guests—a pang of guilt swept over her. Would her parents be ashamed of what had become of their beautiful home? It was their pride and joy, and she sure hadn't done the place right. It had seemed far too much responsibility at the time for an eighteen-year-old girl. It just would've been too hard to keep the bed and breakfast up after they'd passed. Not knowing how to run the business, she'd closed the doors on the historic Hemlock House that fateful summer, and locked herself inside while she'd mourned her parents for a full year.

Entering the bright kitchen, she punched the brew button on the coffee pot she'd prepped the night before and made her way to the pantry to fill Zeke's bowl. He followed behind her, tail wagging in anticipation. Just like every other morning, he ate while she brewed coffee, then they both went outside where she drank her coffee from the swinging bench on the front porch while Zeke wandered around the massive corner lot to greet passersby as they took their morning walks through town.

"Good morning, Mrs. Travis, Mr. Travis." She waved to the elderly couple who lived down the block. They always took their morning stroll at the same time each day, hand in hand.

"Good morning, sweet Emma," they both said in unison before reaching over the white picket fence to pet Zeke.

"Going to be a beautiful day," she called out to them.

"Already is." Mr. Travis smiled and waved before retrieving his wife's hand and heading on their way. She watched them as they slowly disappeared down the block, and a jarring thought took over. Would she ever have a love like that? Or was she going to die alone in this big ole house? She dismissed the thought as soon as it came. *That's silly to worry about at only twenty-six years old.* Surely, she'd find love someday. Right now, she was too busy with her growing business to date anyone seriously. Of course, she occasionally spent time with Aaron Reynolds, a local attorney, but something just seemed to be missing from their connection. So far, things had never gotten past the occasional dinner-and-a-movie phase.

She glanced at her watch and called out to Zeke, "I have to get to work, boy. Come on inside." She put her coffee cup on the antique gossip bench that sat inside the foyer, and grabbed her purse. She gave Zeke one final pat before giving the front door a hard pull to try to latch it shut. She gave it three good shakes to the left and one more to the right before she finally heard it click. Just one more thing to add to her growing list of home improvements.

Emma made her way down Main Street toward NovelTea Books and Tea House, her business that sat only a few blocks from home. She loved the short walk through town every morning to get there. Main street was shaded by mature trees that lined the road, with historical homes adorned with meticulously manicured yards. Colorful flowers hung from pots on each porch, and the smell of sweet honeysuckle filled the air. At the end of the road, Lake Michigan glistened in the distance.

Once she made her way into town, a sense of pride rushed through her as she rounded the corner to see her business awaiting her arrival. Of course, Rose, her best employee, was already inside getting started on the baking for the morning rush of regulars who'd come in for a latte or one of their delicious baked goods that NovelTea was known for. One thing Emma got from her mother was a love for baking, and growing up, that's something they'd always enjoyed together. So, when she opened her bookstore, it was only natural that she would add a bakery inside of it.

"Good morning, Emma," Rose greeted her.

"Quiet morning, huh?" Emma asked, observing that there was only one customer sitting alone at a table by the window.

"Oh, it's just that time of year. Kids are back in school, and most of the summer tourists have gone back downstate."

Rose was only trying to make her feel better, but the sad reality was the business was taking a hit. It was true that Arbor Shores was a seasonal town, but this year her sales were down even more than last September. With a mound of bills piling up on her desk, she needed to find a way to bring in some extra income for the slower months ahead.

"Well, it's only going to get worse when winter hits and the tourists stop coming up on the weekends altogether." She grabbed an apron from the rack and slipped it over her head, tying it at the waist.

"Nah, we have plenty of local regulars who will still be here during winter. Try not to worry about it." Rose put down the rag she was holding and placed a comforting hand on Emma's arm. Rose was a widow in her sixties and had been with her since she opened NovelTea. She was the first person Emma had hired for her new business, and the closest thing she had to a mother figure. Rose loved NovelTea almost as much as Emma. So much so that she worked six days per week, and always arrived early each morning to start the baking; Emma couldn't adequately express the depth of her gratitude for Rose.

Problem was, if business didn't pick up, she wouldn't be able to afford to keep Rose on staff, and letting her go was the last thing she wanted to imagine. Rose was a fixture at Novel-Tea, and the customers loved her witty banter and warm presence. She got to know each customer personally, and always went out of her way to make sure life was easy on Emma. Emma wouldn't have known what to do without her, so the thought of not having her around was one she was unwilling to entertain.

"Hey, how about we run some advertising in the *Beacon*?" Rose suggested. "We could put a coupon in it."

"Don't worry. I'll think of something." Emma flashed Rose her most confident smile and attempted to swallow the ball of uncertainty that had formed in her throat.

Chase Knox punched the throttle on his motorcycle and took the winding back roads at top speed. The crisp northern air felt good on his face, and he was enjoying the ride into Arbor Shores. Sweet nostalgia came flooding back, and he tried not to allow the hint of dread he was feeling over returning home to mix in with it.

Bittersweet.

That's the only word that could describe his arrival. On one hand, he loved it here and had almost forgotten how beautiful Northern Michigan was, especially this time of year when fall was fighting its way into summer. The tall evergreens that lined the country roads filled the air with a familiar aroma, and off in the distance he could see the cobalt-blue waters of Lake Michigan glistening as his bike climbed to the top of each rolling hill. Wouldn't be long now and he'd be arriving in his hometown. So far, this place was even better than he remembered, or maybe it's just that you don't appreciate somewhere until you've had a chance to miss it.

On the other hand, he'd left at just eighteen and hadn't been back since. Now, in the wake of his father's heart attack, it was as good a time as any to come home. The uncertainty of not knowing if his family would accept him tugged at him. Would anyone be happy to see him? Or would they be upset that they hadn't been able to get ahold of him when his father was in the hospital last month? He was probably still the family outcast he'd always been, and he was in no rush to find out the answer to that question.

Growing up, his relationship with his father had never been good. Chase was always the black sheep, the bad boy of the family. His father never approved of his lifestyle or his decisions. Carter Knox was tough on him; even tougher than he had been on the rest of Chase's brothers, although it was all relative. Carter hadn't been easy on any of them. Back then, Chase couldn't wait to turn eighteen so he could get out of Arbor Shores and away from his father's controlling rule and hair-trigger temper, and that's exactly what he'd done as soon as he'd finished high school. Sure, the past eight years had been hard, but boy had he lived. As a drifter, he'd done his fair share of traveling, and had mastered just about every blue-collared vocation possible as a means to survive.

Chase didn't have the same talents his brothers possessed. Shane, his oldest brother, was a famous rock star, and music had always been his passion. His youngest brother, Hunter—filled with business sense and ambition—was the one who'd gone into the family business, Knox Enterprises, which suited him. And his twin brother, Ethan, was a pro football player. Now, that surely had to make their father proud. But Chase had never done anything to make Carter Knox proud. In fact, if his father found out where Chase had been for the past six months, he'd probably disown him altogether, *if* he hadn't already. But that's a secret Chase planned to keep hidden—a secret nobody needed to know about. One he planned to take to the grave.

Would his father or brothers even be happy to see him after all these years? That, he would find out in time. After his twelve-hour trek from New York, right now all he wanted was a cold beer.

He knew just the place.

CHAPTER 2

"What'll you have?" the heavy-set, bald bartender asked, leaning forward against the bar top to get a better look.

"Just gimme a Bud draft," Chase told him, looking around to take in the place. Ripples Bar and Grille had always been the town attraction, and from the looks of it, it was still busy as ever. Although he'd never been old enough to drink there before he left, he'd sure had his fair share of fun out back on the beach behind it.

The man poured a pint from the taps behind him, and set it down in front of Chase, taking his cash off the bar. Chase took a long guzzle, and set down the half-empty glass about the time the bartender brought his change.

"Thirsty, eh?" the man asked, studying him. "You aren't from around here, are ya?"

"What makes you think that?" Chase didn't feel like answering any questions.

"You just have that passing through look about ya. Plus, I ain't ever seen ya before."

"Yeah, just passing through, but might be here a few days."

"Name's John. They call me Big John around here." The bartender held out his hand to shake, and Chase stared at it for a moment.

"Chase," he finally said, and returned the shake.

"You staying at the resort?" he asked. Man, this guy was nosy. There had to be someone else who needed something; the bar was half full already, and it was barely noon.

"Nah, I'm hoping to get a room at the Hemlock House. If they have one open."

"The Hemlock House?" Big John chuckled, and the old man two barstools down joined him. "That place has been closed for years."

"Eight years at least," the old man chimed in.

It made sense, considering Mr. and Mrs. Woods had passed long ago. "So, Emma closed it?" he said to himself, perhaps not as quietly as he'd thought.

"You know Emma Woods?" Big John asked.

"Old friend." Chase downed his final gulp of beer and slid his empty glass toward John, tossing a couple of dollar bills beside it. "Do you know where I can find her?"

Big John folded his arms across his chest but didn't answer. He had a protective look about him, and Chase suspected he wasn't going to tell some stranger passing through where Emma was. Chase had to appreciate that about him. The old man down the bar, on the other hand, was more than forthcoming.

"Oh, you'll find Emma at her bookstore, NovelTea Books and Tea House, right in town. She's there every day."

A smile tugged at the corners of Chase's lips. So, Emma owned a bookstore. That suited her. She'd always been a book-worm, the brains out of the two of them. That's how they'd become such close friends in the first place. In seventh grade, they were paired together for a science project. She was not happy about it at first, thinking Chase was just going to make her do all the work so he could get his easy A. But after class one day, as he walked her to her locker to carry their display, some boys started making fun of her, calling her four eyes for the clunky glasses she always wore. Chase turned around and punched the biggest of the three boys square in the nose, and the other two ran off. Nobody messed with her after that. From that point on, they stuck together and were quite the odd pair, but it worked for them because they were both loners who tended to keep to themselves. She was the quiet, book-smart type, and he was the rebellious bad boy, always in and out of trouble.

By the time they got to high school, they were best friends, and he'd watched her blossom the summer she turned sixteen. He continued to watch out for her as the boys began to take notice of her, and he kept them in line like a protective brotherly-type. The summer they turned eighteen, her parents were killed in a boating accident. He stayed in Arbor Shores long enough to attend the funeral with her, but he left right after and hadn't seen her since. But man, he sure couldn't wait to see her now. He could use a familiar face, and hers was the only one he was ready to see.

"You want another?" Big John asked.

"Nope." Chase got up and gathered his leather jacket and helmet from the stool beside him. "Thanks," he nodded to the old man before heading for the door.

He was on a mission, and there was only one person in this town he wanted to see.

"A little more to the left," Emma heard a voice behind her instruct, but if she swung around on the ladder, she'd surely lose her balance.

"I'll be with you in a moment," she called out over her shoulder, still struggling to get the specials board hung straight behind the counter. She leaned forward, a full three feet of counter between her ladder and the wall, making it a far reach, one that she was growing used to, yet that didn't make it any easier to hang the board each day.

"Allow me," she heard the voice growing near. It sounded familiar enough, but she couldn't quite place it. Whomever it was, she didn't need his help, she just needed a minute to get the board situated so she could get off this ladder. She'd never been fond of heights, and even being a few feet off the ground made her nervous. But she wouldn't allow Rose to get on the ladder with her bad hip, so it had become her least favorite daily task.

A hand reached around her and grabbed the bottom of the board, straightening it on the nail. Whoever it was, he had to be tall to reach without a ladder. But still, she didn't appreciate a customer coming behind the front counter. Swinging around instinctively to see who it was, her weight shifted, and the top of the ladder began to topple to one side. Panic raced through her body, knowing she was going down with it.

She closed her eyes and tightened her grip on the ladder, preparing for the fall. The warmth of strong arms wrapped around her body, scooping her away from the ladder just as she lost her balance. With her eyes squeezed tight, she was afraid to open them until her feet were planted firmly on the ground. Luckily, within a matter of seconds, she was stabilized and quite sure she was standing upright. Slowly opening her eyes, she was greeted with a familiar face only inches from her own, his arms still wrapped tightly around her body.

She blinked hard. Was she seeing things? Could it possibly be? Feeling assured of her balance now, she pulled back and the man loosened his grip, allowing her to get a better look at him as she assessed her savior.

"Chase, is that you?" she asked the man standing before her, his identity partially hidden behind aviator sunglasses. He sure resembled her long-lost friend, but this wasn't exactly how she remembered him. If this was Chase Knox standing behind her counter, he sure had grown into a man—a far stretch from the lanky eighteen-year-old boy he was the last time she'd seen him. Sure, he'd always been good looking, he was a Knox after all and every one of those Knox brothers were known for their looks, but this guy standing before her was ruggedly handsome in his faded blue jeans and black leather jacket. His chiseled features were prominent, even under the five-o'clock shadow and bronzed skin. If it was Chase, she needed to extinguish the flames building inside her. She'd never looked at him like that before, and she sure didn't plan to start now. He was just a friend, a good friend. Well, he had been anyway … until he'd left her.

"It's me, Em," he told her as he removed his sunglasses, revealing familiar eyes. Her heart sped with excitement as she threw her arms around him, taking in the comfort of an old friend as she held onto him for a moment longer than she'd anticipated.

He returned the embrace and a mixture of leather and masculinity hit her nose, his scent new and yet still comforting. He smelled good, and an unfamiliar feeling jolted through her body. She loosened her grip and stepped back to take another look at him.

"What are you doing in Arbor Shores?" Was all she could manage to get out as she studied him. As happy as she was to see her friend, seeing his face brought memories with it— memories of her parents' funeral, and memories of him leaving town right afterward when she'd needed him most. A pain stabbed at her heart with the thought. She'd held onto sadness for a few years after he'd left. How could he have left her at a time like that? But it had been almost eight years since all that, so she decided those questions could wait. That was a conversation for another time. Right now, she'd put that resentment aside to find out what he was doing here.

"That's a question I don't have a short answer for. Have time for a coffee break?" he asked.

She looked around at the handful of people in the store— nothing Rose couldn't handle. "Sure, let me just ask my gal to come take over the counter." She poured two cups of coffee from the pot behind her and slid them to Chase. "Grab us a table."

Taking the ladder into the back, and thankful it hadn't toppled over or crashed into the bakery case, she found Rose kneading dough. "I know this is bad timing, but would you mind handling the counter for me? An old friend just arrived, and I'd like to catch up with him for a few."

"Him?" Rose raised a brow as the corners of her mouth formed into a grin.

"It's not like that. We're just friends," she told Rose, who wore a look that said she wasn't buying it. "*Old* friends," Emma added as she removed her apron and smoothed at the tendrils that had sprung loose from her ponytail.

"Mm-hmm." Rose wore a suspicious grin, but Emma ignored it. She was used to people thinking there was something more between her and Chase back in the day, but there never had been. They were just the best kind of friends.

Sure, she'd grown close to a few girls in town over the past few years like her good friends Avery and Rylee, but in middle school and then well into high school, it had always just been her and Chase. If it wasn't for him, she wouldn't have had many friends in school. She was the one that was known for studying and keeping to herself, but she knew Chase was extremely smart. He'd worked hard to keep that hidden from the world, instead cultivating a carefree, bad boy image. But Emma knew the real Chase. That's probably why their bond was so strong. They didn't open up to most, only each other. There had never been any expectations between them, or catty arguments that most high school friends had, and that was refreshing. They'd do their own thing most days, but then have the most fun when they'd spend time together. And if they'd needed each other, the other was always there. By the time graduation hit, they were closer than she'd ever imagined she could be with another person. That's probably why it hurt so bad when he left.

But again, she'd resolved not to think about that. Right now, she just wanted to get out there and learn what he'd been up to over the past eight years. She'd tried to find him on social media many times, but he didn't appear to have a profile. Knowing how Chase always liked to keep to himself, she wasn't surprised. Eventually, she'd get all those questions burning inside her answered and find out why he'd left so abruptly, and more importantly, why he'd never come back.

Chase looked up from stirring creamer into his coffee to find

Emma walking toward the table. She sure looked different now; more grown-up than he remembered. Although she had always been mature in mind, now her appearance had matured as well. She had started to blossom in high school, and he'd watched her morph from a brainy bookworm into a girl that started to turn all the boys' heads. He'd always resolved not to look at her in that way, but it got harder and harder the older they got—especially once the hormones began to kick in.

Still, he'd never let on that he had any attraction toward her. She was his only true friend, and he hadn't been willing to jeopardize that. But looking at her now, he was reminded of those feelings that began stirring in high school. She'd turned into a woman, and even more attractive than her looks was all that she'd made of herself.

"Chase Knox, I'd all but given up on ever seeing you back here. What brings you home?" she asked, taking her place across from him.

"That's a loaded question." He shot her a playful grin, but he'd have to come clean with her. This was Emma he was talking to. "You heard my dad had a heart attack?"

"Yes, but that was a month ago. I know Shane was hoping to see you then."

"You speak to my brother?"

"He's marrying my good friend, Avery. Didn't you know?"

"No, I didn't." He scrubbed at his face. "Wow. I always knew they'd end up together someday. So, does that mean he's back in Arbor Shores?"

"He sure is," she told him. "Haven't you spoken to him?"

Silence fell between them for a moment. "No," he finally said, looking down at his hands. He was excited to hear his older brother was back home. He just wasn't sure if the feeling would be mutual.

"So, what about you? Are you married yet?" Changing the subject, he glanced at her left hand. Although he wasn't sure why, relief flowed through him when he found her ring finger bare."

"I am, actually."

His stomach dropped. "You are?"

She waved a hand at the tables and bookshelves around them. "I'm married to my business."

He let out the breath he'd been holding. "It sure is great. And it suits you." He reached across the table and gave her hand a light squeeze. "Your parents would be proud of you, Em."

Her smile fell at the mere mention of her parents, and her eyes glazed over for a moment. He shouldn't have brought them up, but it was the truth. They had loved their only daughter dearly, and they'd be proud of the woman she'd become. What he really wanted to tell her was that he was proud of her, too. But he'd swallow that admission for now.

"So, where are you staying?" She took a sip of her coffee.

"Don't know yet. I was hoping to stay at Hemlock House, but I heard it's been closed."

She gave a half laugh. "I closed Hemlock House the summer my parents ..."

"No worries, I'm sure there's another room in town," Chase was quick to change the subject. "I should probably grab a paper to see what's for rent."

"How long are you here for?"

"Don't know yet. That all depends on how my family reacts to my return." He pushed his coffee cup away from him and leaned back in his chair. "I'm in no rush to let them know I'm here, so if you could keep it between us for now, I'd appreciate it."

"In a town as small as Arbor Shores?" she chuckled. "Good luck with that."

"I know, but I just need some time to get settled first."

"Well, don't check into the resort then or you'll run into Shane."

"Thanks for the heads up." He looked out the window. "Do you know of any rooms for rent? I'm relying on a small nest egg to keep me afloat until I can find some work, so nothing too expensive."

Her eyes lit up. "I have an idea."

"Uh-oh, I know that look." He smiled. She had the same look in her eye she'd had when they were fifteen and she'd had the idea of a campout on the beach to try and catch the Northern Lights. They'd both told their parents they were going to a slumber party. Instead, they'd taken sleeping bags out to the shore and built a fire to keep warm. They'd stayed up all night waiting for the show, which did not disappoint. For a quiet, girl-next-door type, she'd had an adventurous side that few knew about, and he'd loved that about her.

"I have an empty guesthouse behind Hemlock House. Mind you, nobody has stayed back there in years, and it probably needs a good cleaning. I suppose I could rent it to you. In exchange for your stay, the Hemlock House just needs a few repairs." Her eyes were filled with excitement and hope.

"You mean, I'll be your on-site handyman in exchange for staying in the guesthouse?"

"Why not?" she asked. "It's just a studio though. You'd have to come inside Hemlock for use of the kitchen, but you'd have your privacy out back."

"Define 'a few' repairs."

"Well, quite a bit of repairs, actually, but nothing you couldn't handle. You were always handy. Thing is, I don't have the time nor the extra cash to hire a contractor, and I'd like to get the place fixed up a bit. In case I decide to sell it someday." She looked around somberly. "Things have been kind of slow around here lately."

He grinned. "This doesn't sound like a bad gig."

"Well, you should know, Hemlock House is not what it used to be. I mean, there's no homemade breakfast in the mornings. It's just me and Zeke, so I don't do much cooking. I'm here most of the time anyway."

"Who's Zeke?" he asked. Did she have a kid he didn't know about? A live-in boyfriend, perhaps?

"Oh, don't worry. You'll love him. So, are you in?" She held her hand across the table to shake on their agreement.

"You've got yourself a deal." He shook hers back and smiled, and something passed between them with their touch. He wasn't sure why, but the thought of spending time with Emma shot life back into him and filled him with an excitement he hadn't felt in a long time.

Especially since the last six months of his life had been miserable.

CHAPTER 3

"**Z**eke, say hello to Mr. Chase," Emma told the excited Lab who was dancing inside the front entrance of Hemlock House.

"Ah, Zeke is your dog," Chase said, taking a knee to pet the dog on his level.

"Well, of course. Who did you think he was?"

"Never mind," Chase said as Zeke snuck in a lick to the side of his face.

"I think he likes you," Emma beamed.

"Most dogs do." He gave Zeke a good ear scratch before getting up to take in the place. Emma was right, it was in rough shape. Still a beautiful Victorian, but it had seen better days. This was not exactly how he remembered it. It still adorned the same furnishings and decor, but time had taken its toll on the old house. Right away, he noticed the floors could use refinishing and the wallpaper was peeling at the corners. Chipped paint bordered the window frames and the windows themselves could all use a good scrubbing. He'd surely have his work cut out for him, but it was a small price to pay to have a place to stay, and he enjoyed manual labor—always had. In high school, he'd worked on a farm just outside of Arbor Shores. After he'd left, he'd done construction for a few years in Nashville before moving on to New York City. It always made him feel manly to work with his hands. And that feeling he got when he'd see the finished product? There was nothing in the world quite like it. It sure beat the gigs he'd had in New York. Especially his last job as a bodyguard. But that's another thing he didn't want to think about.

"You know where the kitchen is. Just let yourself in any time you'd like. I keep the door unlocked."

"What do you mean you keep the door unlocked? Living here alone, Em? You can't do that." He'd seen far more than he'd ever wanted to living in a big city like New York. He couldn't fathom her living alone and not locking her door at night.

"It's Arbor Shores; it's fine." She waved off his concern, but he'd revisit that conversation later.

"All right, show me to the guesthouse."

She led him through the house and out the back door, which just like the front door was unlocked. He was going to get her locking her doors before he left town, that was for sure. The guesthouse sat back in the far corner of the lot, behind what he remembered as a lush garden. Now, it was overgrown with weeds and tall grass. Maybe he'd have time to plant some crops while he was here. Although it was late in the season, and he might not still be around for harvest time, but at least Emma could enjoy them after he left.

She reached up and grabbed a key from the ledge above the front door. "Great hiding spot," Chase teased.

"Hey, at least it's locked." She looked back over her

shoulder and gave him a wink before unlocking the door. A hard push from her hip pried it open.

Greeted by the pungent scent of mothballs and must, Chase assessed his new rental. A full-size bed sat in the corner with a floral bedspread that looked straight out of the eighties, and a couch covered by a sheet sat across from it on the opposite wall. There was an old wooden bistro table for two by the window, and a small bathroom and closet at the far wall. It was all he needed.

Emma yanked the sheet off the couch and ran her finger across the table, collecting a layer of dust on its tip. Color flushed to her cheeks. "I'm sorry. It's been awhile since I've been back here. I guess it's in worse shape than I thought. You don't have to stay back here. I'm sure you'd rather rent a room somewhere else. You know, I hear the Evergreen Manor has vacancies."

"Emma, it's perfect." He offered her a reassuring smile. If only she knew where he'd stayed the past few months, she'd realize this place was a palace in comparison.

"Are you sure?"

He reached out a hand and placed it on her shoulder. "I promise, this is nothing a good cleaning can't fix, and I'm just grateful to have a place to crash."

"All right. Well, I need to get back to work so I'll let you get settled." She started for the door. "If you need anything, just call me at NovelTea."

"Hey, Em," he called after her.

"Yeah?" She turned to face him.

"Can I make you dinner tonight?" It was an idea that had just come to him.

"You cook?" she asked with an amused grin.

"I worked as a sous chef for a bit," he laughed, slightly

embarrassed at the admission, but cooking was one of his passions. He just never had a place to do it, or anyone to cook for. "You know, as a way to say thanks for letting me stay here. Plus, I'd love to catch up with you." What he really meant was he'd love to spend time with her. It'd been so long since he'd seen her, and he looked forward to the company.

"I'd like that." She smiled one last time before heading out the door.

Elation surged through him. First things first, he'd give this place a good scrub down, then he'd walk down the street and do some shopping at Callahan's Town Store. Tonight, he'd make Emma a dinner she'd never forget.

For some reason, a strong desire to impress her had taken over him.

Chase found cleaning supplies inside the butler's pantry of Hemlock House, and had his small guesthouse in living condition in no time. Giving Emma's kitchen inside Hemlock House a quick run-through, he found its contents quite bare, which made him wonder what she actually ate in the way of food. She probably ate at work, because there was little to be found in the fridge.

A quick trip to the store would solve that problem, he just hoped he wouldn't see anyone he knew in town. He wasn't ready yet to let his family know he was home, and in a town as small as this one, it would only be a matter of time before it inevitably occurred. He'd deal with that when the time came, but tonight, he just wanted to enjoy a quiet evening with an old friend.

He put on his aviators, hoping they'd disguise his identity

in the store, and made the short two-block stroll over to Callahan's. Man, there was just something about being back home that felt good. People smiled and waved at strangers in this small town, which normally would make him uncomfortable being the private person that he was, but considering the overall coldness he'd dealt with in the city, he found it to be a welcomed change.

Inside Callahan's, he kept his head down and made a beeline for the meat department. He picked out two chicken breasts and then headed to produce to get everything he'd need to make a sauce from scratch. While making his way to the pasta, he caught sight of Old Man Callahan out of the corner of his eye coming straight down the aisle he'd just entered. Chase shifted slightly, angling his back toward the man, and keeping his head down.

"Can I help you find anything?" Callahan stopped in front of Chase, making it impossible to pass him by. Time had taken its toll on the old man. Heck, he'd been old when Chase was a teen, so he must be in his eighties now.

"I'm good, thanks." Chase's plan was to keep conversations to a minimum. He turned his body toward the pasta that lined the shelves and studied his options, hoping the old man would keep moving.

"You know, I don't understand why they started making all these different kinds. Now you have wheat, gluten free, and even vegetable pasta. Can you imagine that? This one right here is the best, in my opinion." Callahan reached a weathered finger and tapped the front of a box of thin spaghetti noodles.

"Thanks." Chase nodded and grabbed the pasta off the shelf, tossing it into the handbasket he was carrying and turning toward the checkout.

"Son, why do you look familiar? You live here in Arbor Shores, or are you up from downstate for the weekend?"

Callahan was a few strides behind him. He was sure he could lose him if he tried; the old man wasn't moving quickly at all, but Chase didn't want to be rude. "Just passing through," he said over his shoulder while keeping his pace, careful not to turn around to face him.

"You need anything else?" Callahan called out. He always was overly helpful. You couldn't come into this store without Callahan trying to help you shop. It was funny to see that hadn't changed after all these years.

"Nope, I've got everything I need here."

"Well then, let's get you rung up. I'll take you over here at this register."

There was only one other register open, and the cashier had three people in line. Callahan stood behind the vacant register and waited, his brows pinched together, while he studied Chase's face as he approached.

"What did you say your name was?" he asked as he began picking items out of the basket and punching keys on the old register. Why had he never upgraded to a computer system? Not a thing had changed in this store. It was like traveling back in time.

Chase wanted to lie, to come up with some common name like Mike or John, but he didn't have it in him to lie to Old Man Callahan. He'd lied to him once when he was twelve, when he'd been caught swiping a pack of gum. Callahan had promised not to call his parents if he'd come clean. He'd told the truth, but the disappointment in the man's face was enough to ensure he'd never take anything that wasn't his ever again. And he never had. In fact, it was that defining moment that made Chase an honest man. One thing he hated more than anything was a liar or a thief.

"Chase," he finally admitted, almost under his breath.

"Well, I'll be darned," Callahan said with a chuckle and stopped ringing the groceries. "You're Chase Knox, aren't ya?" He leaned in and peered over his glasses, giving Chase a closer look through squinted eyes.

"Yes, sir." And just like that, Chase felt twelve again. He looked around, hoping nobody had overheard their conversation. To his delight, nobody was looking in his direction except the old man staring him down across the counter.

"Well, welcome home, son. What are you doing in town? Nobody around here's seen the likes of you in years."

"Like I said, just passing through."

"Well, I hope you'll stay awhile. I'm sure your brothers will be happy to see you. You know, Shane is back home, too. We have our very own rock star living in Arbor Shores now, can you believe that? I sure am proud of that boy. He's come a long way."

"He has." Chase slid the contents forward on the counter, hoping to remind Callahan to keep ringing. He was growing uncomfortable and wanted to get out before anyone else recognized him.

"What 'bout you? What have you been up to? You married? Have any children?"

"No, sir. Just been traveling a lot."

"Well, where are you staying while you're here?"

Chase would have to think fast. Telling Callahan would be like telling the town all at once over a loud speaker, and everyone in Arbor Shores would not only know he was here, but would know where to find him before day's end.

"I found a guesthouse to rent here in town." That part was

the truth, Callahan didn't need to know *whose* guesthouse. "I really do need to run though. How much?" he asked, quick to change the subject.

With any luck, he'd pay and get out of there without any more questions.

The day dragged on for Emma as she watched the clock impatiently. Business was slow, and she couldn't wait to get home and catch up with Chase. Boy, it sure felt good to have her friend back in town. She'd grown used to living alone, but it could get lonely in that big old house. Zeke was good company, but not much of a conversationalist. The thought of having someone there when she got home from work was comforting, and the fact that Chase was cooking dinner was an added bonus. She laughed to herself. The Chase she'd known didn't cook. It would be interesting to learn where he'd been for the past eight years and what all he'd been up to.

"Why don't you go on home, Emma. I'll lock up here." Rose must have picked up on her angst.

"No, you don't have to do that, Rose. Thank you, though."

"I don't mind. It's only another hour. I know you're anxious to get to that man."

Emma's cheeks pricked with heat. "It's not like that, Rose," she told her with a frown.

"Mm-hmm," Rose responded in her all-knowing tone. Nothing slipped by this woman.

"That noticeable, huh?"

"You've only checked your watch a million times in the past three hours."

"It's just that I haven't seen him in a long time. He's a good friend."

"Well, that's how all the best loves start, you know?" Rose untied Emma's apron and pulled it gently over her head. "Jack and I started out as friends, and we were married for thirty-two years." She tossed the apron on the counter and twisted at the ring she still wore on her left hand.

Emma's heart went out to her. "I didn't know that."

"Oh, yes, we were just friends at first. And it wasn't as common back then as it is nowadays."

"So, what happened?"

"Eventually, it evolved into more. Once I gave in to the inevitable. My only regret is that I fought it as long as I did. If I hadn't, we would've had more years together."

That admission gnawed at Emma. Rose missed her late husband dearly.

"All I'm saying is stay open to the possibility of what could be. I saw the way that boy looked at you today. And I saw the way you looked at him, too."

Rose was seeing things. She and Chase had just been happy to see each other. Surely, Rose hadn't seen what she thought she had. Besides, Chase would be gone again soon. He already said he wasn't staying, so there was no way Emma would be open to anything more. He'd already left her once, and he would be leaving again, but this time she'd be prepared for it.

"Well, I promise you, we are just friends. However, I'll take you up on that offer, if you're sure?"

"Get on home." Rose smiled, and Emma grabbed her things and headed for the door.

CHAPTER 4

The sweet aroma of tomato sauce and Italian herbs filled Hemlock House. That was an unfamiliar greeting upon opening her front door, but one Emma could get used to. The greeting she was *expecting* was from Zeke, but he was nowhere in sight. Where was that dog, anyway? He always met her at the door each day.

"Hello?" Emma called out. She stopped to listen to the tap of nails on hardwood as Zeke came barreling through the house from the direction of the kitchen. "Hey, boy. There you are." She scrubbed at his ears.

Chase appeared moments later. "Welcome home," he said, a welcoming smile on his face. It was clear he'd taken a shower and gotten cleaned up; he wasn't in the same clothing as earlier. Still a T-shirt, but this one was snug on his arms and chest, and it was showing just how much he'd grown into a man since the last time Emma had seen him.

"Well, aren't you a sight for sore eyes. I can't remember the last time I came home and smelled home-cooking coming from my kitchen. It smells fantastic." Actually, she could remember. The last time she'd smelled home-cooking, her parents were alive. Her mother was a fantastic cook and made home-cooked meals almost every day. Nostalgia swept over Emma, twisting at her stomach.

Chase tossed the kitchen towel he'd been carrying over his shoulder and held out his hand to Emma. "Allow me," he told her, motioning for her to take his outstretched hand. Intrigued, she placed her hand in his as a sensation ran up her arm. She let him guide her into the dining room where he already had the table set. "You get comfortable and relax," he told her as he pulled out her chair so she could sit. He promptly filled her glass with red wine before retreating to the kitchen.

I could get used to this. But she'd better not. Chase was only a temporary guest, or tenant, or whatever he was. Point was, he'd be leaving soon, so she wouldn't allow herself to get used to having him around. Though, she *was* starving. She may as well enjoy the perks of his company while she could.

Chase returned from the kitchen with two salads and placed one in front of Emma. Picking up a pepper grinder, he asked, "Fresh ground pepper, *madam*?"

"Sure, *monsieur*," she played along. "Where did you get these proper serving skills?"

"I spent eight months waiting tables in a fine dining restaurant when I first moved to New York," he admitted, taking his place across from her.

"Is there anything you haven't done in the past eight years?" she asked with a grin.

"Very little." He took a sip of wine. Somehow, she believed there was more truth to that than he was letting on.

Emma started on her salad, taking a moment to study

Chase in between bites. It was hard to believe it had been eight years. Being with him was the most natural feeling on earth. It was like he'd been here all along. Yet, in some way, he was different now. More cultured, more grown-up, more mature. It was exciting and comforting all at the same time.

"So, what about you?" he asked. "What have you been up to since I last saw you?"

"Not much around here, as you can see." She motioned around the room. "I spend most of my time at NovelTea. I opened it a couple of years after my parents passed."

He paused and gave her a knowing smile. "I'm sure you miss them."

"Every day." She put down her fork and took a sip of wine, looking out the window. The sun was sinking low in the sky and it filled the yard with an amber glow. She loved this time of day.

"You sure you never got married? I find that hard to believe."

"No," she half laughed. "Who has time for that?"

"A boyfriend?"

"There's someone I spend time with, but it's not serious," she admitted. Which reminded her, she had plans with Aaron this weekend. For some reason, that didn't sound as enticing as it should've now that Chase was here. Maybe she could get out of it. She wanted to spend as much time as possible with Chase before he left again, and there was no telling when that would be.

Chase shifted. "Are you ready for the main course?" he asked when she moved her salad to the side.

"I can hardly wait to see what you've made."

Chase disappeared into the kitchen and returned several

minutes later with two plated dishes of chicken parmesan, placing one in front of Emma before taking his seat.

"This looks incredible," Emma said, wide-eyed. She took a hot bite, flavor and gooey cheese exploding in her mouth. "Mmm, mmm," she indulged. "You keep cooking like this and I'm never gonna let you leave."

"Well, don't get too used to it. I wouldn't want to break your heart when I go." The words jolted her back to reality. *Like you did before?* She wanted to say, but she swallowed the emotion that was bubbling to the surface. That was a conversation for another time.

Emma seemed to be enjoying her dinner, and Chase was happy that he could at least do something nice for her for letting him stay in the guesthouse. He sure did appreciate it, and spending time with her was the most fun he'd had in a long, long time. Over dinner, they'd reminisced about good times they'd had together, and some of their memories had them laughing more than he had in months.

"Are you finished?" he asked, rising to his feet, ready to clear her plate out from in front of her.

"I'll get it." She stood up. "You did the cooking; the least I can do are the dishes."

"Well, I'll help. I'm afraid I've made a bit of a mess in the kitchen." That was an understatement.

"That's a small price to pay for a meal like this. It was delicious by the way. Thank you." She cast him a warm smile that lit up her entire face. Man, had he ever missed that face. It was even more beautiful now than he remembered. All he'd had to remember her by was her senior picture that he carried in his wallet. He loved that picture of her in her blue sweater. While he'd pulled it out and thought about her on more than one occasion over the years, it paled in comparison to the Emma standing before him. To the woman she'd become.

Emma took one step into the kitchen and stopped in her tracks, causing Chase to bump into her. As he did, he got a whiff of her sweet shampoo, sending a warmth through his entire body.

"What happened in here?" She laughed as she turned to face him.

Heat flushed to his cheeks. She was right, he had made a mess of her kitchen. "I'll take care of it. Please go relax; you worked all day."

"I have an idea." A smile formed at the corners of her mouth as her eyes lit up.

"What's that?" he asked, taking her plate out of her hand and moving toward the sink. No dishwasher in this old house, so he'd have to do it by hand.

"The sun is getting ready to set. Let's skip this mess and take a walk on the beach. When's the last time you watched the sun dip into Lake Michigan?"

"It's been far too long." He hated to leave the mess in the kitchen, but something about walking on the beach at sunset with Emma was calling out to him. The kitchen wasn't going anywhere.

"Come, Zeke," she commanded to the dog who hadn't left Chase's side. The two had bonded that afternoon, and Chase was glad to have had the company. He loved dogs but was never able to have one growing up—his father didn't like animals—and he moved around too much over the past few years to have one of his own.

Zeke and Chase followed Emma through the house and

toward the front door where she grabbed Zeke's leash and latched it on. A warm glow lit up the sky out front, and as they walked past the old Hemlock House sign that still sat in the front yard, he noticed she had permanently nailed a No Vacancy sign across the front of it.

"Hey, Em," he asked, falling in stride next to her as they met the sidewalk. "Have you ever thought about reopening the Hemlock House?"

"No," she responded quickly.

"Well, you mentioned things have been slow at NovelTea lately. I just thought that might be a way for you to make some extra income. Hemlock was always the most popular B&B in town."

"It was popular because of my parents," her voice dropped. "Besides, I don't have time to run a B&B. I'm at NovelTea every day except Sundays because we're closed. Running a B&B is a full-time job."

"Well, I just thought—"

"Chase, it's a bad idea." She looked straight ahead, and he could tell the conversation was making her uncomfortable. He decided to drop it for the time being.

"Okay, okay," he put his hands in the air innocently. "Hey, race you to the shore? For old time's sake?" The shoreline was only a block away, and they had always raced there together when they were younger.

A smile spread across her face as she took off down the street, Zeke picking up his pace to keep up with her. Chase loved how Emma was always up for anything. She was a refreshing change from the women he had spent time with over the past few years.

They reached the lake in record time, Chase letting Emma

and Zeke take the lead. "Hey, you two beat me," he told her with a wink.

"I think that's the most exercise Zeke has gotten in years. He's doesn't have much energy anymore."

"Well, do you bring him down here ever?" he asked as they both stopped to kick off their shoes, the cool evening sand under their feet. "He looks energized to me."

She frowned. "Not as often as I should."

The three of them fell in stride once again as they made their way down the shoreline. The sun was low, close to the horizon, the sky ablaze with colors of orange, yellow, and magenta. It was a beautiful evening for a walk on the beach as the waves lapped the shore at their feet. Chase had traveled all over, but he'd never seen a sunset that compared to those in Arbor Shores.

Emma stopped and plopped down in the sand, Zeke making himself comfortable to her left. Chase took a seat to her right as they stared out over the cobalt-blue water.

"Man, it sure is nice to be back here."

"Yeah? Did you miss it here?" Emma asked, drawing hearts in the sand with her finger.

"Not really," he admitted. But as soon as the words slipped out, he almost regretted them. "I mean, not so much Arbor Shores, but I did miss you."

She looked over at him and met his eyes. "You did? Then why haven't you kept in touch?" She was close now, sitting only a foot away, and seeing her up close was doing something inside of him.

"I guess it was the way I left. I felt foolish for up and leaving the way I did."

"Yeah," she said quietly, wiping at the sand on her outstretched legs.

Should he apologize for leaving when she needed him most? It was something he had always regretted, but he'd had no choice. He fought with himself on whether to bring it up, or save it for another time.

His phone buzzed in his pocket. Normally, he'd let it go to voicemail, but he welcomed the interruption while he searched for the right words for Emma.

With the glare of the evening sun blinding the screen, he clicked and answered before seeing who it was.

"Is this my long-lost brother?" said the voice on the end of the receiver.

"Shane?"

"A little birdy told me you were back in town."

"Well, a little birdy told me the same about you. How've you been?"

"Never been better. So, when were you going to tell us you were here?"

"Just got here, man. I was going to tell you. Just trying to get situated first."

"Where are you staying? We can put you up in the resort if need be."

"Yeah, I heard you and Avery were back together. That's great. Actually, I'm staying with Emma."

"Really?"

"Well, not exactly. I'm renting her guesthouse. But listen, we're in the middle of something. Can I call you back later?"

"Sounds good. Wasn't sure if this was still your number since nobody's heard from you, so I was glad when you answered."

"Yeah, about that … I'll explain when I see you." He was just relieved his brother wanted to speak to him at all. He could only hope the rest of the family would be as welcoming as Shane. "Hey, Shane, do me a favor. I'm not ready to let the town know I'm back yet, so if you could keep it between us, I'd appreciate it."

"Well, with Old Man Callahan knowing, it won't be long before the whole town knows, but your secret is safe with me."

"No secret. I'm just not ready to do the family thing yet. Speaking of which, how is he?"

"He's doing better from what I understand. I don't get over there much if you know I mean."

"Got it."

"I sure would like to catch up with my bro, though. Tomorrow?"

"Sounds like a plan. See ya."

Chase hung up and shoved his phone back into his pocket. "Sorry about that."

"No worries. Shane, I take it?"

"Yeah. Good news travels fast, I suppose."

"I told you it wouldn't be long before the whole town knew you were here." She shifted and looked over at Chase. "Why is it a secret, anyway?"

"It's not a secret. I'm just not ready to face my family yet." Chase picked up a rock and skipped it across the top of the calm water. "Truth is, I don't know how happy they'll be to see me since I've stayed gone for so long."

Emma placed a hand on Chase's knee. "I'm sure they'll be happy to see you."

"I'm not so sure," he started. "They might be bitter I didn't come home last month when Dad was in the hospital."

"Yeah, why is that?"

Chase didn't want to lie, not to Emma at least. He prided

37

himself on being an honest man, but there was no way he could tell her the truth. He was already feeling inferior from being back here and seeing all she'd accomplished for herself since he'd left. What did he have to show for the past eight years? Not much. Just his motorcycle and the clothes in his duffel bag.

He took in a deep breath. "I was out of the country. I didn't get the calls until I was back. I came as soon as I found out."

"Really? Where were you?"

He had to think fast. "Costa Rica." It wasn't a total lie. He had spent six months in Costa Rica, just not the *last* six months. The past six months he'd spent in a place that couldn't be any more opposite of paradise. He'd tell her the truth, eventually. Maybe. He sure didn't want to lie to Emma, but this wasn't the time nor the place to tell her truths as hard as the ones he'd lived.

"Wow, really?" Her eyes lit up, and she shifted in the sand to face him. "You amaze me, Chase. You've done so much since you left. I've never even been out of the country. So, what were you doing there?"

"Em, can we talk about it another time?" That's all he had to say to her. Emma wasn't the prying type and would respect his request to let it go.

"No problem." Her eyes turned back to the water and she leaned back on her elbows in the sand. That's one thing he loved about Emma. If they wanted to talk about something, the other would listen, and if they didn't, the other wouldn't pry. It was the best kind of friendship and one he'd missed dearly.

As the last bit of sun escaped into the lake before them, Chase stood and held out his hand to help Emma up. She placed her hand in his, and he pulled her to her feet. Her hand felt so soft and natural in his; he held it for a moment longer than expected. She looked down at her hand and then up a Chase, locking eyes. He quickly dropped it and broke her gaze. "Ready to head back?"

"Yeah, someone has to clean that kitchen," she teased. And the three of them headed back up the shore.

CHAPTER 5

*E*mma woke the next morning, not to Zeke's familiar tongue on the side of her face, but to the smell of bacon lingering through Hemlock House. She opened her eyes and looked around. No sign of Zeke. That was odd. But if there was bacon cooking, she had a good idea of where she'd find him. After a quick shower, she made her way to the kitchen where, to her delight, she found Chase cooking breakfast, Zeke not far from his side.

"Good morning," Chase greeted her. He opened the cabinet next to the sink and fetched a cup for her coffee, taking a moment to pour it for her before presenting it with a smile.

"It smells heavenly in here." She took the mug from him and wandered over to the counter to steal a slice of bacon from the plate next to the stove. She hadn't smelled the aroma of breakfast filling the Hemlock House since her parents were alive. Her mother had always made a large spread for the guests each morning, and by the looks of it, Chase could be feeding a houseful with all that he'd prepared.

"Where'd you get all of this?" she asked.

"Apparently, Callahan's opens early on Saturdays. I took a shot and walked down there. Oh, and your neighbor two doors down sells fresh eggs. They have a chicken coop. Did you know that? Nice couple." He turned back to the stove and the scrambled eggs he was scooping into a serving bowl.

Emma looked at the spread before her in amazement. "Chase, you don't have to keep cooking for me."

"Hey, I like to eat too, ya know." He gave her a wink and handed her a plate. He genuinely looked like he was enjoying himself. She made herself a plate from all he had set out on the butcher's block, just like her mother used to do. They made their way into the formal dining room. Normally, she didn't eat breakfast. She'd have her coffee and go straight to work. After the morning rush, she'd have a muffin or scone—whatever was left in the bakery case.

"I'll get started on the house today. Do you have the supplies?"

"There are some tools in the garage. I don't know what all my dad had back there. I do need to buy some paint and stain though. We should probably go into the city to get that."

Chase took a bite of bacon. "When would you like to go?"

"NovelTea is closed on Sundays, so that would be the best time. Are you free to go with me tomorrow?" She looked up from the toast she was spreading with jam.

"Hmm, let me check my busy calendar and I'll get back to you," he joked. "Of course I'll go with you. It's a date."

Shoot. That reminded her. She had that event with Aaron tonight. It was a mixer put on by the local Chamber of Commerce. As much as she'd love to cancel with Aaron and stay home with Chase, business had been slow at NovelTea lately, so she couldn't really afford to miss a mixer. She usually got one or two bakery orders each time she attended one.

"Speaking of dates, I have plans tonight, so no need to make dinner or anything." She could swear she saw Chase's face drop.

"A date? Anyone I know?" he asked between bites, not looking up from his plate.

"Maybe. He went to school with us but was a few grades ahead. Aaron Reynolds ring a bell? He's the local attorney here in town now."

"Aaron Reynolds is who you're dating?" he asked, his fork hovering over his plate.

"I spend time with him occasionally. It's nothing serious." Why did she feel like she had to answer to Chase? And why did his demeanor shift at the mention of Aaron's name? Did he know him?

"No worries. I planned to meet up with Shane anyway."

They ate in silence for the rest of the meal. Something had shifted, and she wasn't sure what, or why.

After a quiet breakfast, Emma went to work, and Chase cleaned the kitchen before heading out back to the garage to see what all Emma's father had by way of tools. He was pleasantly surprised to find there was just about every tool he could possibly need and more in that old dusty garage. He had a feeling Emma hadn't been back there since Mr. Woods had died. The door had been practically sealed shut.

Chase got busy sanding down the trim on the windows.

He'd start there so they'd be ready for the fresh paint once they got it from the city.

Aaron Reynolds. He couldn't believe it. Figures he'd be an attorney now. Of course Chase remembered Aaron. How could he forget? Aaron was the overachiever in high school—vale-dictorian of his class, student council president—but as Chase remembered him, brownnoser extraordinaire. When Chase pulled the fire alarm before midterms, it was Aaron, who happened to be walking out of the science lab, who'd snitched on him and nearly got Chase expelled from school. If it wasn't for being a Knox and his father's power, he surely would've been kicked out of Arbor Shores High. And although he'd escaped trouble at school, the wrath he'd received from his father was far worse.

But why was the thought of Aaron and Emma together plastered in his mind? Was that a lightning bolt of jealousy that had hit him at the table when Emma said Aaron's name? It had made him seethe inside. The thought of Emma dating Aaron made him feel inadequate, which was silly because Chase and Emma were just friends.

Even if Chase was interested in her, he could never get a girl like Emma. It figures she'd be dating an attorney. That's the kind of man a smart, successful woman like Emma should be with anyway. They were probably a good match. Just one that left him feeling nauseated to think about.

Chase hadn't liked Aaron back in high school, and he had no desire to see him now. He'd have to finish up for the day and get out before Emma came home from work, which made it as good a time as any to go see his family.

$\sim$

"So, how was your evening?" Rose asked Emma after the morning rush had died down.

"It was nice. Chase cooked us dinner, and then we took a walk on the beach."

"Hmm, sounds romantic." Rose looked up dreamily before shooting a smile in Emma's direction.

"It's not like that, Rose. I swear, we're just friends."

"Does *he* know that?" she asked with a pitched brow.

"Well, of course. We've always just been friends."

"When you were kids maybe." Rose went back to kneading the dough for the bread she was baking. "A man doesn't cook for a woman unless he's interested in her. That's all I'm saying."

Was Chase interested in her? No, he couldn't possibly be. She'd heard him; he needed to eat, too. It's not like he was just cooking for her. It had been nice, though, to have home-cooked meals in the Hemlock House again. If she had someone to cook, she possibly could reopen the B&B. But she'd not only need someone to cook but to also keep the grounds and help with the guests. She could never do it on her own. But the extra income could only help since she owned the house outright.

Nah, that was an impossible dream. What if she failed? What if it wasn't as great as it was when her parents owned it? She'd be laughed out of town. Plus, she was needed at Novel-Tea. She couldn't be in two places at once.

"So, what do you and your *friend* have planned for tonight?" Rose asked.

"Nothing. I have plans with Aaron tonight."

Rose dropped the dough on the cutting board and looked up at Emma. "Well, then, now you'll know."

"What do you mean?" Emma asked, not sure what Rose was talking about.

"You bring Aaron Reynolds around Chase tonight, and how he reacts will tell you if he has any interest in being more than just friends."

"Fine," Emma agreed. "I know Chase, and he won't have any problem with me going out with Aaron. I'm telling you, he's not interested in me like that."

"Like I said," Rose added and went back to kneading the dough. "We'll see."

After sanding down all the windowpanes on the lower level, Chase got to work stripping the floors. His plan had been to finish up for the day before Emma got home from work. He would get cleaned up and away from Hemlock House before Aaron showed up. Aaron was the last person Chase wanted to see, especially with Emma. Something about the two of them together didn't sit right with him.

Maybe it was the music blaring from the portable radio he'd found in the garage. Perhaps it was the hard work that had him feeling so good that he'd lost track of time. But somehow, he'd let the day slip away from him, and when he looked up, Emma was standing in the opening of the parlor … with Aaron right beside her.

Chase quickly walked over and flipped off the radio, brushing the sweat from his brow with the back of his hand. Inadequacy bloomed in his chest as he looked from his fitted white tank top and ripped blue jeans to Aaron's dress shirt, tie, and pressed slacks. He and Aaron couldn't be any more opposite.

"Chase, I didn't expect to see you here. I thought you'd made plans with Shane today," Emma said. Zeke sauntered over to greet her, and after a quick ear scratch, moved right past Aaron and took his place back by Chase's side.

"Tonight," is all Chase could manage to get out.

"Chase Knox?" Aaron asked through squinted eyes, peering to get a better look.

"The one and only," Chase answered dryly, quickly going to work to tidy up the room that he'd been tearing apart all day. Should he go over and shake his hand? Nah, Aaron probably wouldn't want to touch Chase's sweaty hand anyway. Probably too afraid he might get dirty.

"You didn't tell me you had Chase Knox doing work here," Chase heard Aaron say under his breath.

"Actually, I'm staying here." Chase stopped and squared his shoulders, folding his arms across his chest.

"He's staying in the guesthouse," Emma quickly corrected.

"Really?" Aaron didn't look pleased. "I didn't know you'd come back to Arbor Shores. Seems all of you Knox boys are returning."

"Please excuse me. I just need to go change," Emma said, heading for the stairs. Leaving Chase and Aaron alone in the parlor.

"Get you something to drink?" Chase asked, his best attempt at being polite.

"No, thank you." Aaron said, his tone cold. He took a step closer. "So, you're staying in the guesthouse?"

"That's right." Chase unplugged the power sander he'd been using, and stared Aaron down as he wrapped up the cord.

"What have you been up to? I don't think I've seen you since high school."

"No, you haven't." Chase ignored his question. The last

thing he was going to do was engage in small talk with Aaron Reynolds.

"So, you've kept in touch with Emma? How'd you end up staying here?"

"Emma's a close friend. Always has been." Chase reached down and scratched at Zeke's head, who still remained loyal by his side. It was odd that Zeke hadn't acknowledged Aaron. He acted like he didn't know him or didn't trust him, one of the two. Either way, that wasn't a good sign.

"That's funny, she hasn't ever mentioned you two were close," Aaron said. Was he throwing a jab?

"Likewise."

The look on Aaron's face told Chase that admission had taken him aback.

"Oh?" Aaron pitched a brow. "That's odd, because we are *very* close."

Aaron's words stabbed at Chase. Another man in his place, close to his Emma? "Well, I have to get going. You two enjoy your night." Chase headed toward the back door and Zeke followed. "You have to stay here, boy," he told him at the door. "I'll see you tomorrow."

Chase slammed the door hard behind him and made a beeline for the guesthouse. He had to get a shower and get to Ripples to meet his brothers. The last thing he wanted to do was think about Emma and Aaron.

Emma made her way down to the bottom of the stairs to find Aaron peering out the side window as if to look in the backyard.

"What are you doing?" she asked.

"Ready?" He quickly turned around and ignored her question.

"Where's Chase?"

"He said he had to go." Aaron stood with his hands shoved into his pockets. "Why didn't you tell me he was staying here?"

"Well, for one, you just met me here and we haven't had time to talk yet. And also, I didn't know it was any of your business, frankly." She surprised herself with how that came out, but she didn't belong to Aaron, and she didn't appreciate him asking. She had every right to have a houseguest. Even if it was a ruggedly handsome houseguest that would make any man feel insecure in comparison. She tried to put herself in Aaron's shoes. What would it be like to find the girl you'd been seeing with a hottie like Chase fixing up her house? It had to make him uncomfortable. Chase was a manly man who worked with his hands, and his bulging muscles and cut upper body hadn't hid that. Aaron had never once offered to help her with any of these projects, so it served him right. She doubted he even knew how to work a power tool in the first place.

"Well, forgive me for asking, but how long is he here for?" Aaron was not letting up, and it was beginning to annoy Emma.

"I don't know. A while, I hope. He's a good friend, and I'm enjoying having him around." She grabbed a shawl from the coat rack by the door and wrapped it around her arms. "Plus, he's fixing up the house for me. In case I decide to sell it."

"Sell it? Well, you have a long way to go if you plan to get this house in selling condition." He looked around the room, digging further and further under Emma's skin.

Her lips pursed together. "Well then, I may just have to

keep him around even longer. Ready to go? I don't want to be late."

"After you," he said, holding the front door for her as she walked through, then closing it firmly on the elephant in the room behind them.

CHAPTER 6

*C*hase pulled his motorcycle into Ripples' parking lot and removed his helmet. A mixture of nerves and excitement swirled inside him. Two of his brothers, Shane and Hunter, were awaiting him inside. It was just too bad his twin, Ethan, wouldn't be inside. He played pro football for the NFL and the season had already started.

Thinking about each of his brothers' successes only illuminated his own faults. That's one reason why he'd stayed gone for so long. He hadn't wanted to come back until he'd made something of his life. But when would that have been? It had already been eight years, and he still didn't have anything to show for himself except for a handful of stories too wild for anyone to believe, his motorcycle—which he cherished—and the shirt on his back. Sure, he'd acquired some skills over the years, but he didn't possess any of the special talents his brothers did. He'd always been the black sheep, the outcast, the drifter of the family, and he wasn't sure how he'd answer questions about where he'd been or what he'd been up to. He figured he'd just answer on the fly. But there were some things he wasn't ready to talk about, not even with his brothers, that he planned to keep to himself.

Chase made his way inside and looked around. There was no sign of his brothers by the bar so he headed out back. In the corner of the patio, they flagged him down from a table by the railing, overlooking the beach.

Not knowing how his presence would be received, Chase reluctantly made his way through the maze of tables on the outdoor patio. He was thrilled at the sight of his brothers, but were they as equally pleased to see him?

"Chase, it's so good to see you, bro." Shane was the first to get up and greet him with a big hug.

"Good to be home," Chase said, patting his brother on the back. He turned to Hunter, who'd also risen to his feet.

"Nice to see you, Chase. It's been far too long." Hunter also leaned in to hug him, and it was a relief. So far, so good, anyway.

"Man, sit down and tell us what you've been up to. We tried to get ahold of you last month when Dad had his heart attack. We left several messages." There it was, the inevitable conversation he'd been dreading.

"Yeah, about that. I was out of the country in Costa Rica. I lost my phone down there, and figured I'd wait 'til I got back to the US to get a replacement. When you called, I didn't have a phone with me and no way to check my messages." Chase hated to lie, especially to his brothers, but he had no choice.

"No phone? I can't imagine," Hunter chimed in, looking up briefly from the email he was checking on his.

"That's because you are always on yours." Shane shot him a look, and Hunter put his phone down and pushed it to the side.

"All right, all right. No business tonight. My phone is off limits," Hunter agreed.

"I came as soon as I got a new phone and heard your messages. Sorry I couldn't be here when you needed me."

"Not your fault, man. You didn't know. We're just glad you're here now," Shane said, putting a hand in the air to get the server's attention. "Can we get a round of beer, please?" he asked as she approached.

Once the waitress took Chase's order and left to get the drinks, Hunter asked, "What were you doing in Costa Rica, anyway?"

"I went down there on a guys' trip. A few guys I worked with were always talking about how great it was. I learned to surf while I was there and fell in love with the area, so I didn't come back with them. I stayed and got a job in Jaco, a beach-side town on the Pacific coast. I took tourists on eco-tours—zip lining, volcano tours—that sort of thing." That part was the truth. All of that had happened, so he didn't feel quite as bad about his words. The only thing was, that had happened three years ago, not in the past six months. He just couldn't tell his brothers where he'd been more recently. He was already feeling like a loser in comparison.

"Man, that sounds awesome. I envy you, bro. You've been able to really live and enjoy your life." Shane took a sip of the beer the waitress had delivered to the table.

Chase was shocked at his brother's admission. "You're a famous rock star. You've got the life all men dream of."

Shane looked out at the water. "Yeah, but it's not all it's cracked up to be."

"So, what are you doing now? Are you still with your band, Distant Union?"

"Oh yeah, we have a tour scheduled for next summer. Just taking some time off until after Avery and I get married. I just needed a bit of a break, you know? I've cut back; just taking it one day at a time."

"That's cool. So, you're in Arbor Shores now? Permanently? And congrats about you and Avery, by the way."

"Yep, this is home base now. I hope you'll consider sticking around awhile. Our wedding is in December, and I'd love to have you stand up as a groomsman."

Chase hadn't thought that far ahead. December was still three months away, which seemed like an eternity. "I don't know how long I'll be in town, but I promise to come back in December for your wedding, how's that?"

"Well, where are you off to next?" Hunter asked.

"I'm not sure." Chase took a drink of his beer, trying to buy some time to contemplate his next words. Truth was, he didn't know where he'd be going next. The only thing that was certain was that he wasn't going back to New York.

"Well, you could always stick around awhile, you know. We'd love to have you back home for a change." Hunter sounded genuine. This was going far better than expected, and Chase was happy to be there, but he wouldn't stay. There was nothing for him in Arbor Shores. Small town life was a refreshing change for a getaway, but it didn't suit him for a permanent home. Or did it? A vision of Emma sitting across the dinner table from him, eating a meal he'd prepared for her, flashed through his mind. That's a thought that he could get used to.

The guys stayed on the patio catching up until the sun had dipped beyond the horizon. Since they'd enjoyed two more rounds of beer, Shane called Avery to pick him and Hunter up.

Out in front of Ripples, as they waited for Avery and were saying their goodbyes to Chase—who had decided he'd walk the few short blocks back to Hemlock House—Hunter added, "So, when are you going to get over to see Dad?" The question had likely been burning in both of his brothers' minds.

"I'll get over there soon," Chase assured Hunter. But Chase wasn't in any hurry to see his father, and he didn't want to go there alone.

"I was thinking, what if I have a barbecue tomorrow afternoon? As a welcome home to you? I could invite him over then."

"Hey, a Sunday barbecue at the lake house sounds great to me. Count Avery and me in," Shane added.

It sounded good to Chase, too, because he had no desire to go to Knox Estates alone to visit his father. He'd far rather have his brothers around for that reunion.

"That sounds good, but I have plans to go into the city with Emma. I'm helping her fix up Hemlock House, and we need to get some supplies."

"How about you do that in the morning, and we'll barbecue around 3 p.m. Sound good?"

"All right, that should work. Let me just make sure that works for Emma."

"Ah, Ms. Emma, huh? What's going on there?" Shane teased.

"Nothing. You know Emma and I are just friends. She's renting me her guesthouse behind Hemlock."

"Emma's a great girl; you might want to reconsider your stance on your 'friendship,'" Shane advised.

"Well, she's out with Aaron Reynolds right now, so I'm pretty sure she's already taken."

"Aaron Reynolds? That guy was in my class. He's a tool. He's got nothing on you, Chase."

"It's not a competition. Like I said, we're just friends." Chase's jaw tightened. This interrogation was beginning to annoy him.

"Yeah, well, let me know when you come to your senses. It's obvious Emma was always crazy about you. I'm sure if you wanted it to be more, it could be."

"No, she wasn't. She doesn't look at me like that. And like I said, she has a boyfriend."

"I see Emma a lot. She's good friends with Rylee. She never talks about Aaron, and she never brings him around. I don't know how close they actually are," Hunter added.

Shane put his hand on Chase's shoulder. "All I know is, that's a girl worth fighting for. You, my little bro, just need to up your game."

"All right, it's time for me to head home. I'll see you guys tomorrow." Chase ignored Shane's comment and left his brothers standing in the parking lot, waiting for their ride. He didn't appreciate their meddling about his relationship with Emma. They were just friends. As far back as he could remember, people had never been able to accept that there was nothing going on between the two of them. There never had been.

Why would things be any different now?

Emma cut her evening short with Aaron. After an hour and a half at the mixer, she'd told him she wasn't feeling well and asked him to take her home. Actually, she was feeling fine, she just wasn't feeling *him* after his interrogation about Chase, which hadn't set well with her. As the evening went on, there was an unspoken tension between them, and she just wanted to get home.

When she arrived, she was disappointed to find Chase's motorcycle wasn't parked in front of the garage. She went in, got into her pajamas, and went to the kitchen to make herself a cup of chamomile tea before bed.

That's when she heard it. There was no denying the sound; she'd lived in that house her entire life. She knew the sound of the latch on the front door being pulled shut hard. "Hello?" she called out. But no one answered. *That's odd.* Zeke was upstairs, waiting for her in bed, so he must not have heard it because he didn't bark or make his way downstairs. His hearing wasn't what it used to be.

"Chase, is that you?" she called again. Still, no response. For the first time ever, she felt unsafe in her home. Had an intruder come into her house? Darn Chase for putting those thoughts into her head. Her pulse quickened as she grabbed a knife from the cutting block and slowly made her way through the dining area, staying close to the wall to stay hidden. When she got to the opening where she could see into the parlor, she held her breath and peeked her head around the corner to investigate.

No one was there.

She tiptoed over to the front door to open it and see if anyone was outside, but when she twisted the handle, it wouldn't turn. That was odd; the door was locked. She didn't lock it when she came in. She never locked the front door. She decided in that moment that she would from now on, but why was it locked right now? Her heart pounded inside her chest.

Someone was in her house.

She turned toward the parlor, and as she did, she noticed

the light of the guesthouse flip on through the side window. *Thank heavens.* Chase was home. She bolted toward the back door as fast as her feet would allow and ran outside, slamming the door behind her. Running through the backyard, hand still gripping the knife, she made her way to the guesthouse and began banging on the door until it swung open.

CHAPTER 7

"*E*mma, what's going on?" Chase asked, his eyes immediately falling to the knife she was gripping, then making their way up her body. He didn't mean to stare, but she was standing at his door in a pair of thin, silk pajamas consisting of shorts and a matching tank, which left little to the imagination.

"Chase, someone is in my house!" She dropped the knife and lunged forward into his arms, and he could feel her silky body pressed against his. He wrapped his arms around her instinctively, as if to shield her from the possible intruder. He held her tight and locked the door.

"You stay here. I'll go over there," he said as he picked up the knife off the floor.

"No! Don't go in there. What if he has a gun? Let's just call the police."

Chase began sifting through the pockets of his leather jacket hanging on the back of the chair. "How do you know someone is in there?" he asked, pulling out his phone to power it on. His plan was to first call the police, and then go in the house and capture the intruder himself. How dare someone try to harm Emma.

"Because I heard the front door shut, and when I went to check it, it was locked. I know I didn't lock it. Someone came in and locked it behind them. Someone is in my house!" Her voice was frantic, and relief flushed through him as he listened to her words. "Why aren't you dialing? Why are you smiling?" she demanded, panic and fear still stricken on her face.

"That was me, Em," he told her, tossing his phone on the table and then putting his hands on her shoulders in an attempt to calm her down. "I was walking home from Ripples and saw your bedroom light on upstairs. I checked the front door and noticed you had left it unlocked. I locked it for you and pulled it shut. I don't like the thought of you being alone in there at night with your door unlocked."

"Chase Knox!" She swatted at his arm. "You nearly gave me a heart attack."

She was still huffing. This look of vulnerability on her face was something he wasn't used to seeing from Emma. She was always so independent and laid back. A strong desire to console her took over him. He pulled her into his chest and wrapped his arms around her, in an attempt to calm her down. "I'm sorry, Em. I was just looking out for you. I didn't know it would startle you." As he held her tight, her arms wrapped around his waist, and she rested her head on his chest. He put his chin on top of her head and held her, the smell of her shampoo tantalizing his senses.

Holding Emma's soft body in his arms was making him feel things you're not supposed to feel for your best friend. As if she'd likewise suddenly discovered the awkwardness of the situation, Emma pulled back and wrapped her arms across her chest, a clear attempt to cover herself.

"Here." Chase picked up on her discomfort, and grabbed his sweatshirt off the sofa, which she quickly pulled over her head.

"I feel like an idiot," she said, plopping down on the couch. "I've lived in that house alone for years and never once have I been scared. It was you who put bad thoughts in my head about leaving my door unlocked. I should have known better. This is Arbor Shores."

"Small town or not, you need to lock your doors." He took a seat next to her. "That's exactly my point; had your doors been locked, this never would have happened," he teased.

She swatted at him playfully, and finally, a hint of a smile turned up the corners of her mouth. Finally, she was beginning to calm down. Problem was, he was getting worked up inside, in a way that was confusing him. She looked just as good in his over-sized sweatshirt as she had standing in those silky pajamas at his front door, and he was finding it hard to take his eyes off her, or shake the feeling that still lingered of having her in his arms.

Emma didn't want to go back inside the main house. Not alone anyway. Now, she was wide awake, and her idea of having a cup of tea and going to bed was long gone.

"What are you doing home already, anyway?" Chase glanced at the clock on the wall. "It's just after nine."

"I'd had enough of the mixer." What she really meant was she'd had enough of Aaron. "I was ready to come home."

"Must have been an exciting date," Chase said dryly.

Was that a hint of jealousy she was picking up on? Nah, Chase didn't care who she went out with. Why would he?

"Hey, I don't really want to be alone after that ordeal, and now I'm wide awake. Wanna watch a movie with me?"

"Are you inviting me inside the main house? I feel so special," Chase said with a grin.

"You can come inside Hemlock House anytime you want. You're always welcome."

"I know. I was only kidding."

"So, how about it?"

"Well, I don't know, I had big plans to finish *Beyond Good and Evil* tonight," he said playfully, motioning to the book on his nightstand.

"Ah, I see you made your way to the upstairs library." Emma was amused. She appreciated that Chase was a closet bookworm; it was something she assumed nobody knew about him except her, which made her feel special. She was pleased to find he'd helped himself to a book from the Hemlock House library. "I think Nietzsche will understand."

"Well, I could probably be persuaded to break away, *if* you had some popcorn."

"I do have popcorn, believe it or not. That's one of the few things I'm sure to keep on hand." She got up from the couch and waited for him at the door.

He rose off the couch to follow her. "All right, but I get to pick the movie," he said, closing the door behind him as they stepped into the cool night. "I remember how terrible your movie-choosing skills are."

"Hey, I resent that remark," she teased back. They had always loved to go to the theater, but Emma was notorious for picking the worst movies possible. Half the time they would get up and leave and go sit out by the lake to look at the sky and try to catch shooting stars. "Okay, you can pick out the movie, but nothing scary. I've had enough thrills for one night."

She could feel Chase's hand on the small of her back as they made their way inside the back door of the main house, sending a tingling sensation straight up her spine. Why was she having this reaction to Chase? It didn't make sense. Still, there was nobody else she'd rather be spending her Saturday night with, and she was grateful for his company.

"I'll go change so you can have your sweatshirt back. Then I'll start the popcorn. You find us a movie," she told him as Zeke came barreling towards them and stopped right in front of Chase. If she didn't know better, she would swear that dog was smiling at him.

"Don't change," he said, bending down to pet Zeke.

"Huh?" she stopped and asked.

"I like the look of you in my sweatshirt." He turned and flashed her a grin. "Keep it."

Heat flushed to her cheeks and she knew they were turning red. He liked the looks of her in his sweatshirt? What was that supposed to mean? That's the first time he'd ever made a comment towards her like that, and oddly enough, she didn't mind it. Plus, she liked the feeling of *being* in his sweatshirt, especially since it carried his scent. For whatever reason, that scent was comforting to her.

Emma headed straight for the kitchen to start the popcorn so Chase wouldn't see the flustered look on her face. She'd just put his comment out of her mind for now. He probably didn't mean anything by it, and she was likely overthinking it. There was no way her best friend was making a pass at her.

After making homemade popcorn on the stove and drizzling it with extra butter—just how Chase liked it—she turned around to find him standing in the doorway of the kitchen, with his hands behind his back.

"Oh, you startled me!" She placed her hand over her heart and took a deep breath. "I've had enough excitement for one night, remember?"

"We have a little problem," he told her, a serious look on his face.

"What's that?" She set down the popcorn and turned to face him, awaiting his response.

"I'm afraid I've made a mess of the parlor. I moved all the furniture today and stripped the floors. We can't watch a movie in there."

"Hmm, well, the only other television in the house is in my bedroom, and I don't—"

"Looks like it's back to the guesthouse we go." As he said those words, he pulled his arm around the front of his body and held up what he'd been hiding behind his back.

"What's that?" She cocked her head to the side to get a better look at what he was holding.

"Only the best movie ever." He moved closer to show her.

"Did you find a copy of *Friday the 13th*? Where did you find that old VHS?" *Friday the 13th* was always their favorite movie, and the only one they'd ever agreed on.

"I found it in the library. And since that old TV in the guesthouse still has a VCR hooked up to it, we can watch it back there."

"I do love that movie. But remember, I said nothing scary?"

"Don't worry, I'll protect you." He gave her a wink.

Another pass? Or was he just being jovial?

"Do you think you can get that old VCR to work?"

"There's only one way to find out."

63

~

Chase, Emma, and Zeke made their way back to the guesthouse, popcorn and VHS tape in hand. Emma made herself comfortable on the couch while Chase fiddled with the VCR. It took some blowing into the old dusty thing, but somehow, he got the VHS tape to play.

He grabbed a throw blanket off the foot of the bed, and sat down beside Emma on the couch, spreading it out to cover her bare legs as well as his own. The couch in the guesthouse was small, so their arms were touching, causing a charge to pass between them. They had to be close to share the popcorn anyway, but having Emma beside him was making it hard to concentrate on the movie.

When the scary scenes would come on, Emma would turn and grab Chase's arm. Was she doing it instinctively? Her actions were sending him mixed signals. As much as he enjoyed the idea that Emma might actually be interested in him as more than a friend, he knew better. She had a stable, successful boyfriend. What would she see in Chase? Besides, would he really want to screw up their friendship? It was a bad idea, and why was he having these thoughts about Emma, anyway? He spent the entire movie fixated on Emma's actions instead of the movie, and by the time it had ended, he was more distraught than ever.

As the credits began to roll up the screen, he looked over and noticed Emma had laid her head back and drifted to sleep. He didn't want to wake her, and he sure didn't want to send her back into Hemlock House after the scare she'd had earlier followed by a horror movie on top of it, so he rose to his feet and scooped her up. He'd place her in his bed, and he would sleep on the couch. It was the gentlemanly thing to do.

Just as he lifted her up and swung around to walk toward the couch, her eyes drifted open.

"What's going on?" she asked through sleepy eyes, her face only inches from his. The only light in the dark room was the glow coming off the TV. It illuminated her features perfectly and he had an overwhelming desire to lean down and kiss her. He'd have to fight the urge with everything he had, because she looked like an angel in his arms, and felt so natural there. It was as if she were meant to be there all along.

He took a deep breath. It would take every ounce of restraint he had in him to keep himself from placing his lips on hers. But as badly as he wanted it, he wouldn't do it. He wasn't good enough for Emma, and he wasn't willing to ruin their friendship to find out if he was the only one feeling something happening between them.

"Shh, go back to sleep. I'm putting you to bed," she heard Chase whisper softly. Emma looked up at his face, so ruggedly handsome and just inches from her own. She could feel his strong arms cradling her body, and she wondered if he was going to kiss her. He'd stopped walking, and he was holding her in the middle of the room, staring down at her. They locked eyes for a moment, before his eyes made their way to her lips. Now she was sure he was preparing to kiss her, and oddly enough, she wanted it. She was ready for it, like she'd been waiting for it her entire life.

Slowly, she closed her eyes, as if to grant him permission. The warmth of his arms, the anticipation of the moment—it sent an influx of yearning through her body, and she parted her lips in anticipation.

A softness met her body beneath her. She opened her eyes to discover Chase had placed her gently on his bed. He turned to grab the blanket from the couch to cover her, while a mix of disappointment and humiliation consumed her. What had come over her? What made her think Chase actually wanted to kiss her?

More importantly, was she really hoping to kiss her best friend?

CHAPTER 8

The next morning, Emma woke early. She looked over and found Chase sound asleep on the couch. She got up quietly and motioned for Zeke to follow as she opened the guesthouse door slowly, as not to wake him.

Once inside the main house, she put on a pot of coffee and headed upstairs for a hot shower. She needed to clear her head. The fact that she'd almost kissed her best friend last night was still ringing loudly in her head. Or was she just imagining things? No, she was sure of it; he had almost kissed her. So, what had happened to make him change his mind? Perhaps it was a moment of weakness. They couldn't go down that road —no way. Not with Chase leaving again, especially. But more importantly, she didn't want to ruin their friendship now that they'd reunited. She wasn't willing to lose him. She also wasn't willing to get too close to him this time around because she knew Chase, and from the sound of his stories, he didn't stay anywhere long. Plus, it had hurt too bad to lose him last time. She needed to keep him at arm's length.

By the time she had finished her shower and got dressed,

she had decided no more late night movies in the dark guest-house with Chase. They'd have to be more careful about the situations they put themselves in. But still, if he was just a friend, why was the feeling of his strong arms wrapped around her body still lingering? Or the way she'd craved his kiss when their lips had been only inches apart? Or the way she'd stayed up half the night because his scent clinging to his sweatshirt was driving her crazy, in the best way possible.

"Em?" she heard Chase call out from downstairs. What was he doing there already? She took a final glance in the mirror. Why did she care what she looked like? They were just going to pick out paint. She never was one for much makeup—she didn't need it—but she grabbed the mascara and applied a thin coat on her dark lashes, and dabbed a touch of gloss to her lips. Giving her long waves a quick tousle, she decided she was ready to face Chase and headed for the stairs where he was waiting at the bottom.

"What are you doing here already? I figured you were still sleeping," she asked from the top of the stairs.

"I heard you leave, and I got up and showered. I figured we'd get an early start because Hunter is having a barbecue today. I was hoping you'd come with me after we get back from the city."

"Hmm, I don't know. I should really get some work done around here today." As badly as she wanted to spend the day with him, it was probably not a good idea while these feelings were stirring inside of her. She needed to keep their time together to a minimum.

"Em, it's Sunday, and you only get one day off per week. How about a little fun?" He smiled as she began to make her descent. "Besides, I'll take care of everything around here. That's my job."

She liked the thought of that. It felt good to have someone helping her take care of things for a change. Not that she needed it. She had managed to take care of herself since her parents passed, and she was doing just fine, but she didn't mind having him around, and she loved that he was handy and enjoyed working on the house.

A sharp pain in her pointer finger ripped her from her thoughts. "Ouch!" she yelled out, looking down to realize she'd finally gotten that inevitable splinter from the railing.

"What happened?" Chase made his way up the stairs to meet her, concern in his eyes.

"I got a splinter. This dang railing ..."

"Let me see." He met her on the middle step and took her hand in his as he inspected her finger. The smell of a freshly showered man hit her nose, causing her knees to weaken.

"Do you have any tweezers?" he asked.

"In my bathroom."

"Come with me." He held her hand and guided her upstairs.

Inside the master bathroom, she pulled tweezers from the drawer and handed them to him. "Be gentle," she said, looking up at him. Facing her, he took a step towards her, not breaking her gaze, and placed his hands on her hips. *He's going to kiss me for sure this time.*

There was a hungry look in his eyes that she'd never noticed before—one she wasn't used to seeing from him. His grip tightened on her waist as he lifted her up. This time, the feeling of his hands on her hips sparked electricity in her body. He placed her down gently on the vanity counter and took a step closer. *Here it comes.* Why was she having this reaction again? She'd just decided she wouldn't entertain these newfound feelings for Chase. And here she was, longing for him to take her in his arms and place his lips on hers. Just like she'd wanted the night before.

Chase looked down at her hand, breaking the chemistry happening between their eyes. He turned her hand over and slowly picked at the sliver in her finger with the forceps. She closed her eyes, not because it was painful, but because the sight of Chase only inches from her face was causing her pulse to quicken, and she was sure he could hear her heart pounding in her chest.

"There you go," he said, stepping back to show Emma the piece of wood captured on the end of the tweezers. She opened her eyes and locked with Chase's. "All better," he said, looking at her with the sexiest of grins on his face. He held out his hand to help her down off the counter, and when she placed her hand in his, another surge passed between them.

She was sure now, something was developing between them. The only question remaining—was he feeling it, too?

Chase and Emma made their way toward the city in her old pickup truck. The ride was long, and Emma was quiet over in the passenger seat. What was on her mind? When he wasn't consumed with thoughts about what Emma was thinking, their evening kept replaying over and over in his head—the way she'd felt so natural in his arms, the way she'd closed her eyes and parted her lips when he'd almost kissed her. Was it just a coincidence? Or was it possible she'd wanted the kiss just as badly as he had?

Then this morning, he'd almost kissed her again in her bathroom. Had she noticed? No, she couldn't have known he was two seconds away from tossing the tweezers aside and scooping her off the counter into his arms, taking her mouth in his.

What had come over him? He had started to develop these feelings for her in high school, but those feelings paled in comparison to the emotions he was experiencing now. He'd have to get a grip and regain his composure. She had a boyfriend, and she wasn't interested in him like that. He would never be good enough for her. He was no Aaron Reynolds.

"I love this time of year," she finally said, breaking the silence between them.

"Why's that?" he asked, relieved that she had initiated the conversation.

"The leaves are starting to get a hint of color. Fall is just around the corner."

"Yeah, I've always loved it as well. Especially in this area. There's no place more beautiful to experience fall than Northern Michigan."

"You would know," she said under her breath, but he had heard her. He'd just ignore that comment for now. Somehow, he had to diminish this tension that had formed between them, not amplify it.

"Hey, I have an idea," he looked over at her.

"What's that?" she asked, still staring out the side window.

"Do you think Gandy's Cider Mill has opened for the season?"

"I'm sure it has. They always open in early September."

"Wanna go?"

She turned to face him, and he could see she had a glimmer of excitement in her eyes now. "I could go for some cider and donuts," she agreed. They had loved driving out there once Chase had gotten his car when he'd turned sixteen. They would go every weekend in the fall until the first snow came, and then the mill would close its doors for the year.

Chase followed the long country road they were on until he saw the sign for Gandy's Cider Mill up ahead. He turned left and the road turned to dirt, mature trees fighting to shade the sun from slipping through onto the dusty path before them. When they got to the end, the old mill greeted them. It was still early in the day, and most people were likely still in church because there were only a few cars in the lot. *Great timing.*

Chase parked the truck and Emma hopped out, meeting him at the front bumper. He held out his hand to her, and she looked down at it, a confused expression on her face. She paused for a moment, before placing her hand in his. He wasn't sure why he'd held out his hand for her, but her soft hand sure felt good in his, so he clasped it until they got to the door. He held the door open for her, and inside, the aroma of fresh baked donuts, old wood, and crisp apples filled the air. Chase ordered them a small bag of cinnamon and sugar donuts, and they sipped on their hot cider while the donuts were made fresh.

Once the plump older lady behind the counter handed over the hot donuts and Chase paid, they headed out back to a picnic table next to the babbling river to enjoy their donuts and cider. Each taking a seat by the water, they sat side by side as they faced the stream before them. Not a person around, they had the back of the property to themselves.

The trees that bordered the river had just started to turn, and boasted hints of red, orange, and yellow. The weather was ideal—low seventies, full sunshine, not a cloud in the powder-blue sky above. The day was perfect. The *moment* was perfect.

Chase took a deep breath and closed his eyes to take it all in. A gentle breeze rustled through the leaves, and the water made a melodic tune as it made its way down the river toward the mill. It was the epitome of peace being there with Emma. He could've stayed in that moment forever.

"This is nice," he finally said, opening his eyes and taking a sip of his cider.

"It is," she agreed. "It's a gorgeous day." She offered him a small smile, and he couldn't help but notice how the sun shone down on her features, illuminating her natural beauty. The attraction he'd had for her the last few days since he'd returned was far stronger than anything he'd ever experienced with another woman. He was dying to know if she felt it too or if it was just one-sided. Should he tell her how he'd been feeling? She was always so easy to talk to, so why was he having trouble finding the right words?

No, he couldn't tell her what he'd been feeling inside. The stakes were too high. If he told her his true feelings, and she didn't feel the same, that would ruin their friendship. He couldn't have that. It was too risky. But if he was ever going to tell her how he truly felt about her, this seemed like the perfect setting to do so.

"Chase, I have to tell you something." Her admission pulled him from his thoughts.

Chase perked up. Was it possible she'd been having the same thoughts, sitting there? Could it be that she was feeling the exact same way, and was about to profess her love to *him*? He took a deep breath and held it as his pulse began to quicken. A sense of relief jolted through him as he anticipated her words. "What is it?"

Emma shifted on the picnic bench to face him, a serious look on her face. "There's something that's been bothering me that I want to talk to you about."

"You can always talk to me, Em. What's up?" He turned

his body toward her to give her his full attention, and now they were facing each other, eyes locked.

"I've been trying to find the right words. I actually considered not saying anything at all, but I have to get this out. I realize it might cause some issues between us, but it needs to be said."

He couldn't believe it. She *had* been feeling it, too. He hadn't just been imagining things. Emma was feeling the same way and she was about to tell him. He couldn't wait to hear those words and to tell her he'd been feeling the same. He took her hands in his and held them. "Just say it," he whispered.

She looked down at her hands in his and took a deep breath before she spoke. "You really hurt me when you left."

He could feel his expression fall. "Huh?" he tried to say, but his voice cracked. Those were not the words he was expecting.

"I'm sure you had your reasons for leaving the way you did, but you left me at a time when I needed you most, and it hurt me. Badly," she added.

"Emma," is all he could manage to muster up. He stood up and faced the river, rubbing at the back of his neck. What was happening?

"I just want to know why you left and why you couldn't have stayed a little longer." He could feel her standing behind him now. "It was the hardest time in my life, and the person who was always there for me disappeared. No phone call. No letter. No explanation. Do you have any idea how bad that hurt me?"

He always carried guilt for leaving right after her parents' funeral, but he'd had no choice but to leave when he did. How would he ever make her understand? He wanted to turn around and take her in his arms and apologize, but that wasn't the solution. He had to be honest with her.

"Chase, look at me." Her voice was closer now.

"Em." He turned to face her, still searching for the right words. They were staring into each other's eyes now, Emma's face filled with hurt and confusion. *Just come out with it. Just tell her the truth.* He took a step toward her and rested his hands on her shoulders, looking deep into her eyes. "I'm so sorry I hurt you. That was never my intention."

"But I want to know why. It just doesn't make sense, Chase. You were always there for me. It was always you and me against the world. And then for you to up and leave when I needed you most, with no explanation? It just hurt, you know?"

"Emma, please sit with me." He walked back to the picnic table and took a seat. He was going to come clean. She followed him and sat down beside him and waited, giving him the space he needed to find the right words. "I had to leave when I did, and I don't expect you to understand since you didn't get an explanation from me. I know it's coming eight years too late, but I hope you'll hear me out."

A beat of silence echoed between them. "Go on," she said quietly.

"My father kicked me out the night after your parents' funeral. I came home to a bedroom full of boxes. He'd had Jeffrey, our butler, pack all my things. He'd said I was eighteen now and had graduated high school, and it was time to get out on my own. He'd said since I refused to work in the family business and hadn't applied to college, I was no longer welcome in his home."

"Oh my, Chase. I didn't know." She reached out and placed a hand on his knee. "Still, I wish you had just told me."

"I was too embarrassed to tell anyone. Even you."

"Well, thank you for telling me now."

He let out a long, exasperated breath. "That's not the end of the story."

~

"He told me I'd never amount to anything." Emma watched the pain manifesting in Chase's face. "He'd said that I was the biggest disappointment he had for a son. That out of all of us Knox boys, I was his greatest letdown. He basically told me to get out of the house and out of his life until I'd made something of myself."

"I had no idea."

"You have to understand, to hear that from your father at only eighteen, it did something to me." He pushed off the picnic table and began to pace. "I felt worthless, humiliated. I vowed right then and there that I would get as far away from Arbor Shores as possible, and I wouldn't come back until I'd made something of myself."

"Chase, you're not worthless." She wanted to get up and wrap her arms around him. She wanted him to see himself through her eyes, even for a moment, but instead she sat there, frozen by his words.

"I wanted to come say goodbye to you, but I made an impulsive decision to buy a bus ticket that night and get out of Michigan. I threw only the necessities in a duffel bag and went straight to the bus station. I wanted far away from this town and everything that reminded me of it. I figured if my father felt that way about me, it must be true. I figured everyone here must feel the same way about me. Even you."

"Chase, I never felt that way about you. And I never gave you any reason to think that."

He walked over and stood in front of her, lowering his voice. "I know, Em. But try telling that to an eighteen-year-old boy who didn't have a future and had a father who was ashamed of him."

"I understand, and I'm sorry I brought it up. I just had to know." Emma looked down and drew a circle in the dirt with her shoe. It was too hard to look at him. Too hard to see the pain in his expression.

"I want you to know something." He sat back down next to her. She looked up and met his eyes. "It killed me to leave, to know you were hurting and alone. I missed you, Em. For a long, long time. But I couldn't reach out. I was too ashamed to reach out to anyone until I'd made something of myself."

"But it's been eight years, and you've done so much now. How come you didn't call or come back sooner?" She still had burning questions inside. He could've kept in touch.

"Because look at me." He threw his hands up in the air. "What do I have to be proud of, huh? What do I have to show for myself? I still haven't made anything of myself. I didn't want to come back until I could prove my father wrong. And now look. Here I am, and I have to go face him today with nothing to show for the past eight years. No wife, no children, no career, nothing." He got up and faced the river again, and Emma could have sworn she saw his eyes gloss over before he did.

"Chase, who cares about those things? That doesn't define you as a man."

"My father does, for one. Look at my brothers. All three of them are successful. And then there's me," he said, his voice clogged with emotion.

Hearing Chase's words, she could feel the pain and humiliation he was holding inside. She never would've guessed that he had any insecurities; he'd always seemed so strong and sure of himself. And here he was, struggling to be back in Arbor Shores and dreading facing his father. There was no way she was making him go to that barbecue alone.

"Well, I don't know if this counts for anything, but I think you're pretty special." She walked up behind him and wrapped her arms around him, resting her head on his back. He didn't turn around, and she knew that was because he didn't want her to see the emotion streaming down his face.

In that moment, all she could do was hold him, and hope it was enough to show him how she truly felt about him.

hase and Emma got to the city, picked out the paint and stain, and made their way back toward Arbor Shores so they could get to the barbecue on time. They had stayed at the cider mill longer than anticipated, and it was now nearly 3 p.m.

Chase's admission at the mill had changed something between them. The awkwardness that seemed to exist earlier that morning was gone, and Emma felt closer to Chase than ever. She'd decided she'd let go of the hurt and resentment she'd held for him leaving and try to understand where he was coming from. Still, she'd never forget the hole it had left in her heart, and she'd be lying to herself if she said she didn't fear it happening again. After finding out the way he felt about being home, she was pretty sure he wouldn't be staying in Arbor Shores, and depending on how the reunion went with his father, he might even be gone sooner rather than later, and that scared her.

Since she was now more certain than ever that he'd be leaving again soon, she made a promise to herself that she would extinguish any flames building inside for Chase. It was unrealistic to develop feelings for someone who would be gone soon. That was a sure path to a broken heart, and one she wasn't willing to take. Besides, she and Chase had just gotten close again, and she wasn't going to ruin it. By the time they got back to Arbor Shores, she'd decided that "just friends" was all her and Chase could ever be.

"Do you want to stop at home and drop off this paint?" he asked as they stopped at the light on Main Street.

"Yeah, I should probably let Zeke out, too," she said.

"Hey, I have an idea." He looked over and smiled.

"What's that?"

"Let's take my motorcycle to Hunter's. It's a beautiful day for a bike ride. I think I saw an extra helmet in the garage you could wear."

"That was probably mine from when my dad would take me out on his." The memory of taking motorcycle rides with her father tore at her heart. She had loved exploring the winding country roads on the back of her dad's Harley.

"So, what do you say?"

She didn't have to think twice. "Sounds like fun."

They pulled into the driveway of Hemlock House and Emma let Zeke out for a few minutes while Chase unloaded the paint. Then, he fetched the extra helmet out of the garage, and cleaned it up for Emma.

Holding it out for her, he smiled as she approached the bike. Man, she looked beautiful, and there was no one he'd rather have behind him on this ride.

He straddled the bike first, and held it stable so she could climb on the back. Emma put her hands on his shoulders to brace herself as she settled in behind him.

"Hang on," he told her as he powered on the bike, flexing the throttle to roar the engine before making their way onto Main Street.

Emma slipped her arms around his waist and held tight, and he could feel the warmth of her body on his back. It felt so good having her arms wrapped around him, just like it had back at the cider mill. He was feeling a bit foolish for opening up as much as he had, but that was the thing about Emma. She didn't judge him, and she was a great listener. She really was the best kind of friend.

They took Pine Ridge Way south of town toward Hunter's lake house. As soon as they got out of the town limits, the evergreen-lined road opened up to a long stretch of winding asphalt before them. Each time they would come to a twist in the road, Emma would lean with the bike, making it a smooth ride. She was a natural back there, and now Chase was convinced more than ever that's where she belonged. Just when he thought she couldn't get any more perfect, she turned out to be a rider. She wasn't scared to get on his bike and had been up for it right away. She was always up for anything.

As they snaked down the coast, parallel to the Great Lake to the right of them, it became clear—Emma was his dream girl.

After a couple of miles, Emma pointed out Hunter's driveway up ahead, and Chase slowed the bike to turn in. After making their way down a long driveway, a massive nautical-style house perched on the shore of Lake Michigan appeared before them. Several cars were already in the driveway, and it was apparent that they might be the last to arrive.

Getting off the bike, they placed their helmets on the seat

and headed for the house. Chase paused at the front door and took a deep breath.

"You ready for this?" she asked.

"Ready as I'll ever be." He forced a smile.

As he did, she looped her arm through his. "Don't worry. I got you." She offered him a reassuring wink, and they made their way inside. Something about having Emma by his side was comforting to him; with her, he could take on the world.

"Hello," Chase called out, but he could see right through the open concept home and the wall of glass on the backside of the house that everyone was out back on the veranda. His brother had sure done well for himself. Hunter's home was large and immaculate. He scanned the crowd through the windows as they made their way through the house. Was his father out there? If so, he couldn't place him. Did that mean Carter hadn't wanted to see him? His heart plummeted at the same time he was hit with a wave of relief. As much as that would hurt, it was also ideal. Nothing could prepare him for coming face to face with Carter Knox after all these years.

As soon as they slipped out the sliders off the back, everyone stopped what they were doing to greet them.

"Hey, you finally made it. We were beginning to think you weren't coming to your own barbecue," Shane said, giving his brother a one-armed hug as his fiancée, Avery, hugged Emma and then turned to Chase.

"Good to see you again, Chase. Welcome home," Avery told him. He hadn't seen her since they were teenagers. She was Shane's high school sweetheart back then, and he could see why his brother had recently reunited with her. She was still as kind and as beautiful as ever.

Hunter closed the top of the grill and walked over. "Welcome. Make yourselves at home."

Rylee came around from behind the outdoor bar she was stocking with ice and wiped her wet hands on her shorts before giving them both a hug. "Chase Knox, it's been far too long," she told him, then hugged Emma before making her way to Hunter's side. Those two made a great couple. Chase never would have guessed they'd end up together, but it worked.

After the inviting welcome, Chase noticed his father and his stepmom, Valerie, sitting off to the side of the patio, under the shade of an umbrella table. Hunter must have followed his gaze.

"Come on; Dad's here," Hunter said. Chase followed his brother as his pulse quickened with each step. Thankfully, Emma didn't leave his side. Somehow, she was making this reunion manageable.

"Dad, Valerie," Hunter announced, "Chase and Emma are here. You remember Emma Woods, right?"

"Of course. Hello, dear," Valerie was the first to speak. She stood up and held out her dainty hand for Emma to shake. Emma said her hellos to each of them, and then Valerie turned to Chase and enveloped him in a hug, which was a bit awkward. He'd never cared for Valerie, especially since she was the reason his father and mother had gotten a divorce when he was a teenager—a nasty and public divorce causing his mother to flee to Florida. Not to mention the humiliation his mother had experienced when all of Arbor Shores learned of Carter and Valerie's decade-long affair. Carter had moved her into Knox Estate, and Chase was forced to live out his teenage years with Valerie taking his mother's place inside their family home.

"Valerie, nice to see you," Chase said as they pulled apart. It was a stretch from what he was really thinking, but he would do his best to be polite. Chase couldn't help but notice his father hadn't moved.

He turned to his father. "Dad," he said, holding out his hand across the table for his father to shake.

Carter looked at his son's hand for a moment, and then extended his own. "Chase, welcome home, son." Carter's words were a shock. He'd not only welcomed him home, but he'd called him *son?*

"Thank you," was all Chase could say. Seeing his father was stirring up all sorts of emotions inside of him.

"Sit down and tell us what you've been doing with yourself these past few years," Valerie said, motioning to the seats across from them. *Great.* The inevitable conversation he'd been dreading.

Chase and Emma both took a seat. "You know, just traveling a lot. That's why I couldn't come sooner. I was out of the country," Chase started. He was hoping there wouldn't be an interrogation of where exactly he'd been or what he'd been doing there. Where he'd really been was someplace he never wanted his father to know, or Carter would surely disown him once and for all. He needed to change the subject, and quickly. "Are you feeling okay, Dad?"

"Ah, it'd take more than a heart attack to take out a Knox," he said, swatting at the air with an aged hand. Chase was sure his words were meant to sound tougher than they'd actually come out. It was odd seeing his father like this. He was older now, and somehow, he seemed smaller, weaker. Chase remembered him as a powerful, middle-aged businessman, always in a suit and tie. Now, his father wore a light pink polo shirt and white shorts and had deep lines etched on his face. He looked to be about twenty pounds thinner than Chase remembered him. Still looked like his father, but perhaps not as intimidating. Maybe the heart attack had aged him a bit. Or perhaps Chase had just been gone too long.

Valerie broke the awkward silence that had surfaced. "Emma, it was a terrible tragedy to learn about your parents. I never got a chance to tell you how sorry I was to read about their accident in the *Beacon*."

"Thank you," Emma said, and took a sip of iced tea that Rylee had brought over.

"I noticed you closed the old Hemlock House. Nobody could blame you at the time. Any plans to reopen it?" Chase was relieved Valerie had changed the subject.

"I don't think so," Emma said. "But Chase is fixing it up for me in case I decide to sell it."

"Is that so?" Carter asked.

"Sure am," Chase responded, looking over at Emma and giving her a wink.

"Well, I sure hope you'll consider reopening it. It's a beautiful home and was so popular in its day," Valerie added.

"It's just too much for one person." Emma looked down at the straw she was twisting in her glass.

"Well, perhaps Chase could stick around and help you," Valerie's words jolted Chase from his gaze on Emma.

"How long are you in town, anyway?" his father asked before Chase or Emma could reply to Valerie's idea. Helping Emma reopen Hemlock House sounded enticing to Chase, but he wasn't sure if he was willing to stay long enough to make it happen.

"I'm not sure yet," Chase said.

"Well, it's good to see you back home," Carter said, and then held up his glass to indicate to Rylee that he'd like another scotch. Carter seemed to have lightened up on Chase, but his entitlement was still intact. The fact that he expected someone to wait on him at a barbecue was typical Carter Knox for you.

Rylee brought Carter a fresh scotch, and she and Hunter joined the table, which was a relief to Chase. That was the end of the interrogation as the conversation shifted to lighter topics and small talk.

Chase was pleasantly surprised with how well the reunion with his father had gone, even though he still held hurt and resentment toward him and he'd never forget the things his father said to him. But after his father nearly died last month, it had put things into perspective for Chase, and he wanted to at least leave things on good terms. Doesn't mean they had to have a relationship, but the way things were left had hung over Chase for the past eight years, and this felt better. His father was actually treating him like a man, and if he didn't know better, he'd think Carter was happy to see him. They might never have the conversation that needed to be had, so Chase could receive the apology he'd likely never get, but he'd take this for now. Heck, maybe he *would* stick around for a while.

It wasn't long before it was time to eat and afterwards the air was starting to cool as the sun was getting low earlier and earlier these days.

"How about I build us a fire on the beach?" Shane asked.

"We'd better get going," Valerie said to Carter, eyeing his empty scotch glass. Chase remembered how Carter's lips would get loose and his temper would flare with too much scotch, and he was relieved to find Valerie seemed to have a grip on it.

Carter and Valerie rose from the table and said their good-byes. There was no hug between Chase and his father, and Chase was fine with it. He wasn't ready to let everything go just yet, and he was secretly relieved when they left.

The three couples made their way through the seagrass and out to the shoreline where Shane had built a fire in Hunter's firepit. They stayed out there for a few hours after the sun dipped into the lake, and the brothers reminisced and told stories from when they were kids as the girls caught up with one another. Shane had brought his guitar and sang a song every so often. It was the perfect end to the evening, and Chase couldn't have been happier to be spending time with his brothers. All that fear that they wouldn't accept him was all for nothing.

Rylee was the first to leave. "I need to get home to Liam," she said. Chase knew Rylee was close friends with Emma and Avery, but he'd just today learned that she was a single mother to a seven-year-old boy and owned a ballet studio in town. She and Hunter had recently gotten engaged and were planning a summer wedding for the following year. Chase was happy that Hunter had Rylee and Liam in his life. It seemed to have humbled him.

"We should go, too," Avery added. "We have to be at the resort early tomorrow. They're installing the last of the solar panels in the morning."

"Solar panels?" Chase asked.

"Yeah, we are doing our best to turn Arbor Shores Resort green."

"That's great," Chase told them.

"Yeah, Shane and Avery are doing big things for the resort. It was just featured on *Traverse City Today*."

"Good for you guys." Chase was happy to learn that his brother had a project to work on with Avery. Something to keep him home and off the music tour for a while.

"I'm going to walk everyone out and then head to bed," Hunter said. "Why don't you two enjoy this last log on the fire." He nodded at Chase. "Stay as long as you'd like. Don't forget Rylee and I are having an engagement party at the resort on Saturday."

"Wouldn't miss it for the world," Chase told him before Hunter headed back toward the house, leaving him alone with Emma on the beach.

When everyone was gone, Chase noticed Emma's bare arms. She looked cold, so he took off his leather jacket and put it around her shoulders.

She looked up at him and met his gaze with a smile. "Thank you."

He took the seat next to her. The sky was dark and dusted with stars, and the sound of gentle waves lapping the shore mixed with the crackle of the fire. An amber glow from the flames illuminated Emma's face, and Chase again felt an over-whelming desire to kiss her.

"Thank you for coming with me today," Chase said. Emma looked up at him and noticed the glow from the fire had put a twinkle in his eye. Something about being out here alone with him—the fire, the water, the stars above—was romantic.

"Of course. I think it went well, don't you?" she asked.

"Better than expected, actually."

"I was surprised that Valerie suggested you stick around and help me reopen Hemlock House," she said. She decided to bring it up and feel Chase out on the idea. She wasn't sure if she would seriously consider reopening it, and she certainly couldn't do it on her own, but she was curious what Chase had thought of the idea, and that curiosity got the best of her. More than anything, she wanted to know if he would ever consider staying in Arbor Shores.

"Yeah, me too."

Emma cleared her throat and straightened her back. "Is that something you'd consider?"

"You mean, you *are* thinking about reopening Hemlock House?"

"To be honest, I hadn't until today. It was never an option because I could never do it on my own. But if you wanted to stick around, we could do it together. Be business partners even."

Chase stared at her, as if in disbelief. He looked like he was contemplating her offer, and the anticipation of his response was making her heart race. Was it even an option for him?

"Wow, Em. I never dreamed you'd ask me that."

"Well, I was just thinking. You're an amazing cook. You could do the breakfast and the maintenance. I could do any baking we'd need down at NovelTea and bring it over. And if the B&B did well, I could even afford to hire another employee at NovelTea to free up some of my time for the B&B." Emma felt hope bubbling up inside of her as the words came out of her mouth. She felt just as surprised at the idea as Chase looked, and as crazy as it was, the two of them together could make it work.

The thought of reopening Hemlock House someday had never drifted far from her mind, she just always thought it wouldn't be feasible—she could never do it alone. But she loved that old house and all it represented in Arbor Shores. Plus, in some way, she wanted to do right by it. To make her parents proud even if they were no longer here to see her run it. They had left it to her, after all, so they must've had hopes that she'd keep it open.

Not to mention, the thought of having Chase stay in Arbor Shores was breathing excitement into her—a feeling she hadn't felt in a long time.

"I don't know what to say." He looked perplexed, and Emma worried she may be asking too much of him.

"Well, you don't have to answer me today. Why don't you think about it?"

"Don't get me wrong, I'd love to run a business with you, and I'm flattered that you'd even ask. I just hadn't thought about staying here permanently. I just need to make sure that's what I'm ready to do, you know? It wouldn't be fair to open the B&B, and then leave you with it. I'd have to make this my permanent home."

"Yeah, I would need a commitment from you before I'd consider it myself. But I sure would love it if you stayed."

"You know I'd love to stay here with you, Em," he told her, placing his hand on her knee, causing ever nerve ending in her body to come alive. "Just let me sleep on it, okay?"

"Take your time," she told him with a smile, and laid her head on his shoulder.

They sat there in silence and watched the last remaining log smolder on the fire until it was time to head back home.

CHAPTER 10

$\mathcal{C}$hase awoke before his alarm the next morning. He wasn't sure if he'd ever actually fallen asleep. He'd tossed and turned most the night, contemplating Emma's offer. The thought of staying and becoming her business partner was a great opportunity. Plus, he loved Hemlock House. Some of his greatest childhood memories happened right inside its walls with Emma and her parents. In a strange way, he felt an obligation to it, just as he was sure Emma did.

The reunion with his father had gone well, and his brothers seemed happy he was home. Being back in Arbor Shores with Emma and his family was going far better than he ever could have imagined, and Chase was starting to think this was where he belonged. Could he give Emma the commitment she deserved? It was not only an opportunity to own a business and make something of himself, but it was also a way to ensure he had Emma in his life forever. But would he be able to handle being business partners and maintain a platonic friendship with her with these feelings that were building inside of him? Should he tell her his true feelings before he accepted her offer? It was the right thing to do, but there was so much at stake. Admitting how he felt could break their friendship apart, and ruin his chance of becoming Emma's partner.

Still, he knew what he had to do.

Chase got a quick shower and then made his way into the main house to begin working. Letting himself in through the backdoor, there was no sign of Emma yet in the kitchen. He decided to put on a pot of coffee for her, and then head to the parlor to get started on the floors.

"Good morning," he finally heard Emma announce behind him.

He turned around to an angel leaning against the doorway, cupping a mug of coffee. "Hey, Em." He paused to take a moment and look at her. The mere sight of her pulled the air from his lungs.

"Thank you for putting on the coffee."

"Anything for you." He winked and stood up off the floor.

"I usually drink it on the porch in the morning. Care to take a break and join me?"

"Sure." Chase dusted his hands on his pants and followed Emma and Zeke outside. He and Emma took their spot on the swinging bench while Zeke made his way down the stairs of the porch to greet the morning walkers.

"So, what's on the agenda for today?" she asked, taking a sip of her coffee.

"Well, for one, I'm sanding down that staircase railing. No more splinters for you." He flashed her a grin. "And I plan to finish the floors today."

"I can't tell you how good it feels to finally get this place fixed up."

"Well, I'm enjoying it," he told her. "In fact, I've given your offer some thought, a lot of thought, actually, and I want to take you up on it. I want to stay here and run Hemlock House with you."

"You do?" She shifted on the bench to face him, excitement lighting up her face.

He turned his body to face her. He needed to be honest with her, and it was now or never. "Yes, but there's something you should know before you accept. There's something I need to tell you."

Emma took another drink of her coffee, the excitement in her face moving to concern. "Go on."

Chase took Emma's hand in his. "Em, I have to be honest with you about something. It's only fair that you know if we're going to run a business together. I don't want our partnership to be awkward."

"What is it? You can tell me anything." She put her mug down on the table beside the bench, giving Chase her full attention.

Having Emma stare at him in anticipation caused his pulse to race. He just needed to come out with it. He pushed off the bench and began pacing the patio, fighting to find the right words. Emma waited patiently until he made his way back to her and took a seat again.

"Okay, here it goes." He took a deep breath and blew it out before continuing, "I started developing feelings for you in high school, and I never told you."

Emma let out a snort. "That's what you needed to tell me?" Her face shone with amusement. "Chase, I had feelings for you in high school, too. Actually, I had feelings for you in middle school, as well, now that I think about it. We were kids; it's only natural that we would be confused about our friendship. We were both filled with hormones." She smiled and picked her coffee back up.

That was news to Chase. He had no idea she'd had the same feelings back then. Had he known, would he have left? He pushed the question aside. Of course he would have. He didn't have a choice. Knowing only would have made leaving hurt worse.

Part of him was relieved to get that off his chest, and the other part of him was slightly hurt that she'd just laughed off his confession. He needed to finish. He'd come this far, so why not just come out with everything?

"But, that's not all," he continued, rubbing at the back of his neck with his hand. "Em, I think I still have those feelings for you."

"You do?" She straightened her back and sat up on the bench.

There was no sense in stopping now. "Actually, I know I do. In fact, I've nearly kissed you a half dozen times in the last few days. I don't know how you haven't noticed."

Warmth rushed to her cheeks. "I don't know what to say."

"Well, please say something, anything," he told her, feeling foolish for confessing his true feelings. He should have known it would go this way. He should have known she didn't feel the same.

Emma was stunned speechless by Chase's revelation. He had been feeling it, too? Should she tell him she had been feeling the same way about him? And that she'd craved that kiss as much as he had? No, not if they were going to run Hemlock House together. If they were going to be business partners, they'd have to remain professional. But still, if she was ever going to tell him her true feelings, this was as good a time as any.

"Well, to be honest, I've been a little confused by these feelings I've been having for you as well." *There*. She'd said it.

Chase cocked his head to the side. "You have?"

"Yes. In fact, I was dying for you to kiss me the other night in the guesthouse. I don't know what came over me, but it's been a confusing time for me as well. You're not supposed to have feelings for your best friend."

"Says who?" Chase asked, and Emma looked up at him.

"I don't know. All I know is that you're the most important person in my life right now. I finally have you back here, and you're the closest thing to family that I've got. I don't want to ruin that, you know?"

"I get that. That's why I was hesitant to tell you. But I thought it was only fair. If we are going to be business partners then you have a right to know."

Emma traced her finger along the rim of her coffee cup. "Well, I think if we are going to be business partners, we should probably try to keep things professional. That would only complicate things. Especially if it didn't work out between us. What would happen then?"

"So, what are you saying?" Chase scrubbed at his face with his hand.

Emma took a deep breath and let it out before continuing. "I'm saying that I'd love to run Hemlock House with you, but I think we should try to push these feelings aside and just remain friends if we are going to move forward with this plan." That sounded good in theory, but would she really be able to do that? She hadn't been able to get Chase off her mind since the moment he'd stepped into NovelTea and scooped her off her feet. Literally.

"Okay," Chase looked down at his hands. "I can respect that."

She placed a hand on his. "Chase, look at me," she whispered and waited until he met her gaze before continuing. "I care about you. Deeply. You're my best friend, but you and I both know we can't go down that road. I appreciate you being honest with me." She died a little inside saying those words, but she knew it was the right thing to do.

He looked up at her and met her eyes with his. "Always."

"So, does this mean you're staying? We're business partners?" She held out her hand to shake on their deal.

He took her hand in his and returned the shake. "Let's do it, partner."

The moment should've been filled with joy, but the ache in her heart overpowered it. Had she really just put Chase in the friend zone? How would she live and work, day in and day out, with him and never have him as her own? Perhaps they were making a mistake. That's something only time would tell.

Right now, she had to get to work.

CHAPTER 11

*T*he week had flown by as Chase kept himself busy fixing up Hemlock House. He was motivated now more than ever so that he and Emma could finally reopen the doors.

By Friday, he had refinished the hardwood flooring along with the entire staircase, re-wallpapered the parlor and formal dining room, and painted all the trim on the windows. It was all starting to come together. He'd worked long hours all week to get it done, and now he was looking forward to an evening with Emma. They had plans to go out to dinner to celebrate the progress of Hemlock House when she got off work, so he put his tools away and went back to the guesthouse to get showered and ready for the evening.

When he was finished with his shower, he made his way back to the main house to meet Emma. To his surprise, she wasn't home yet. He decided to make a snack to hold him over; Zeke stayed close to his side, Chase assumed in the hopes of scoring a bite of turkey.

"Hey, you," he heard Emma announce.

He turned around. "Hey, I was starting to worry about you. I thought you'd be home an hour ago." He took a big bite of his sandwich.

"I would have been," she started as she made her way to the fridge. She opened it, grabbed the pitcher of lemonade and poured them each a glass. "I had to stop by Aaron's office."

It was a punch to the gut. She had plans with him but she'd been with Aaron while he was here waiting? Anger bubbled to the surface, but he'd have to keep his cool. They were just friends, so he couldn't let his jealousy over Aaron shine through. This was something he was going to have to get used to.

"Oh yeah, what for?" Chase asked, ripping off a piece of crust for Zeke.

"I asked him to put together a contract for us. For our business."

Chase nearly choked on the bite he had just taken. "You did what? Why would you have Aaron oversee our agreement?" he asked once he'd managed to swallow.

"Because he's my attorney. What's the big deal?"

"I didn't know he was *your* attorney. I thought he was just *an* attorney."

"Well, he's the best in town, and yes, he's *my* attorney. That's how we started dating, actually."

Chase didn't want to hear about her dating Aaron. He didn't want to hear another *word* about Aaron. But he had to know. He'd imagined Aaron had something to say about this, and Chase wanted to know exactly what that was.

"Well, what does he think of our plan?" he asked, trying to sound nonchalant as he returned the sandwich fixings to the fridge.

"Honestly, he's not thrilled about it. But it's not up to him, so what difference does it make?"

"Well, what did he say, specifically?" Needles pricked at the back of his neck as he waited in anticipation.

"He's just being protective, as attorneys are."

"You mean as boyfriends are," Chase corrected her.

"Aaron is not my boyfriend, Chase." Emma fired a look at him that said she was not pleased with his assumption.

"Yeah," he muttered under his breath. "Well, do you have the agreement?"

"No, we went over the terms and he said he would get started on it. It should be ready on Monday."

Chase didn't like the thought of Aaron overseeing their agreement, but he decided to let it go for now. He wasn't going to let this ruin his evening with Emma.

Emma wasn't pleased with the way Chase had drilled her about Aaron, but she couldn't blame him. If he knew how against their business plan Aaron was, Chase would really be upset. She decided not to tell him that's why their meeting had run over and why she was late coming home. It had caused quite an argument between her and Aaron, and Aaron was convinced she was making a huge mistake. Still, he'd agreed to put the paperwork together—not because he'd wanted to, but because it was his job and she had him on retainer.

After Emma went upstairs to freshen up, she met Chase back in the parlor. "This place looks amazing, Chase. You've really done a nice job with it."

"Thank you," he said, giving her a once-over. She noticed how his eyes scanned her body in her formfitting, black dress.

Was it too much? They'd planned to have dinner at La Fresca's, the new fine dining restaurant in town. It was upscale, so she figured a dress and heels were appropriate. She couldn't help but check out Chase herself. He wore black dress pants and a heather gray button-down shirt. She hadn't seen him dressed up since ... well, ever, and he looked good. Not that he didn't look good in the tight-fitting tank tops and faded jeans he wore most days when he was working on the house, but this was a different look, and he was as handsome as ever. Heat traveled through her body as he made his way next to her and held out his arm to escort her to dinner, the light scent of his cologne intoxicating to her senses.

They said goodbye to Zeke and made their way down Main Street. Everything was a short walk in Arbor Shores, and Emma loved living in the heart of town. In just a few short minutes, they were at the new monstrosity on the water. Emma was pleasantly surprised to find that Chase had called ahead and made a reservation for a table by the window with a clear view of the lake. The sun was starting to set, and the colors emanating from the sky cast a warm glow throughout the room. It was quite romantic, which was making it hard to look at Chase as just a friend. To anyone else around them, they probably appeared to be a couple—a very happy couple, indeed.

The server arrived for their drink order and Chase took the liberty of ordering a bottle of red. He seemed to know his wines and that made Emma realize he had even more worldly experience tucked away that she didn't know about. *That's something that might come in handy for the B&B.*

The server delivered the bottle and presented the label to Chase. He nodded his approval, and the server worked at the cork with his wine key and poured a taste in Chase's glass first; he breathed the aroma in through his nose and then took a sip before approving Emma's pour. She was impressed. This wasn't something she'd expected from her bad boy best friend who'd shown up on his Harley. She appreciated that there were many sides to Chase—sides anyone rarely got to see except her. Something about that made her feel special.

"To Hemlock House." Chase held up his glass for a toast after the server had finished pouring both glasses and had taken their appetizer order.

"To Hemlock." Emma held up her glass to clink with his. "And to us," she added. Chase locked eyes with her as she said it, and she quickly took a sip and set her glass down. She unfolded her linen napkin and placed it in her lap, looking down to smooth out the wrinkles.

"So, when do you think we'll be ready to open?" Chase asked, taking out his own napkin and following suit.

"Well, the downstairs is ready now, thanks to you. The upstairs just needs updating. The rooms have been closed and nobody has stayed in them. They just need a good cleaning, and we should probably update the bedding with new linens."

"I'll get started cleaning up there tomorrow."

Emma took a sip of wine and continued. "I think we will be ready to open by the end of the month. We just need our agreement finalized, and I have Aaron checking to see if we need any permits or licenses updated. I'm sure we do."

Emma noticed Chase's jaw flinch at the mention of Aaron's name. She was sure he was jealous of Aaron, but he'd never say it. If he only knew Aaron had nothing on him in Emma's eyes. She'd take spending time with Chase over Aaron any day.

The server brought their appetizer first, and then their salads. They talked about their plans for getting people to

Hemlock House, and decided they'd try social media advertising to get the word out to people downstate as soon as they
started to generate some income. In the meantime, they'd
attend the Chamber mixers so the locals could help spread the
word. Another thing Emma appreciated about Arbor Shores
was the sense of community, and how everyone was always so
supportive of NovelTea. She was well-respected in town—
people loved her baking and her bookstore, and she was often
asked to supply baking orders for other local businesses. She'd
just have to get Aaron to lighten up on Chase and accept the
fact that she was starting this business with him whether he
liked it or not.

They enjoyed their entrees—Chase a steak and Emma the
lake perch—and then split a small piece of cheesecake with
local cherries on top before finishing their wine and asking for
the check. Emma reached for it. She'd planned to pay for half,
but Chase grabbed it quickly and pulled out cash to cover the
total. It was odd to her to see someone pay with cash anymore,
and she wondered if he even owned a credit card.

Getting up from the table, Chase followed Emma through
the maze of white linen-clad tables as they headed toward the
exit. Side by side now, the comfort of his strong arm sliding
around her waist sent another rush of heat through her body as
they made their way toward the exit.

They had to walk through the lounge to get back toward
the front door, and as they did, Emma saw Aaron get up from
the bar and head towards her and Chase. She sucked in a deep
breath and held it. He was the last person she wanted to see
tonight.

"Surprised to see you here," he said to Emma as he
approached, leaning in to plant a kiss on her cheek.

"Hi, Aaron. You remember Chase, right?" Emma asked, ignoring his comment.

Aaron shoved his hands into his pockets and rested back on his heels, staring Chase down. Chase dropped his arm from around Emma's waist to mirror Aaron's stance, and neither one spoke. You could cut the tension with a knife. He finally gave a nod in Chase's direction, but shifted his focus back on Emma.

"We were just celebrating the progress of Hemlock House. You should see what Chase has done with the place this week," Emma said, looking over at Chase and offering him a small smile.

"Is that so?" Aaron asked, but Emma could detect something in his tone that wasn't sitting well with her. Something she didn't like one bit.

"Yes, he's really fixed it up nicely, so we should be ready to open soon. We were just discussing the details."

"Well, it looks more like you're on a date to me," he told her, folding his arms across his chest.

"I'll see you on Monday, Aaron." Emma refused to give his remark a response. This wasn't a date, was it? And, so what if it was? She didn't belong to Aaron, and she didn't like this new side of him that had emerged ever since Chase had shown up in town. Chase wasn't going anywhere, and Aaron would need to get used to it. "Ready, Chase?" she asked, turning toward the door.

They left Aaron standing in the middle of the lounge. As they made their way through the crowd, she could feel Chase's hand slip back around her waist. This time, she couldn't help but wonder if he had an agenda.

They made their way out into the night and Chase found it was a pleasantly warm evening for September. There was a slight drop in temperature, but luckily Emma had grabbed a shawl before leaving the house, so he thought he'd give his idea a shot.

"Wanna walk home along the beach?" he asked.

Emma looked down at her shoes, and then leaned down to pull her sling-back heels off. "I'd love that."

Chase followed suit, and they made their way toward the shoreline. The sun had fully set, and the moon had moved in its place, casting a silver-blue glow on the sand stretched before them.

"What's Aaron's deal, anyway?" Chase finally asked as they fell in stride, and made their way up the secluded beach. For such a nice night, Chase was surprised there wasn't a soul to be seen besides them.

"He's just overprotective, I guess."

"No, I'm overprotective. He's jealous. There's a difference," he corrected her. But was there? Chase had been secretly jealous of Emma and Aaron's relationship, but he wouldn't tell her that. He saw how she'd reacted to Aaron's jealousy, and Chase didn't want to have her upset with him as well.

"Can you blame him?" she asked, stopping to turn and face him.

Chase stopped walking and turned to her. "What do you mean?"

"Come on, Chase. I have a hot, manly guy practically living with me, who I'm spending all of my time with and who I'm now opening a business with. It does kind of look like we're together, don't you think?"

"So, you think I'm hot?" Chase teased as he wiggled his

eyebrows. But inside, her admission had made his heart skip a beat.

"You know you're hot, Chase. You always have been." She looked down at the sand and dug at it with her toe. Through the light of the full moon illuminating her features, he could see her cheeks redden.

That overwhelming desire to kiss her had returned. He wasn't sure if it was the wine, or the romantic atmosphere of their dinner, or the pull of the moon on his emotions, but something inside of him was telling him it was right. That this was not only the time, but the perfect setting. If it ruined their chance of opening the B&B, well, that's a risk he was willing to take.

He took a step forward, closing the space between them. Reaching out, he gently guided her chin up with his fingers, causing her to look up at him.

"What are you doing?" she asked softly, but her voice shook. Chase knew she was well aware of what he was about to do, and she wasn't doing anything to stop him.

"Why can't we be, Em?" he asked, his voice low.

"Why can't we be what?"

"Together," he whispered, wrapping his arms around her waist and pulling her against him. She didn't fight it or try to break free. Another green light that was fueling his confidence for what he was about to do. He moved a hand to the side of her face, cupping it at first, and then slowly guiding her mouth closer to his.

"But we decided that we weren't going to—"

Before she could finish her sentence, Chase swept his lips across hers. Gently at first, testing her reaction, until her body released the resistance she'd been holding between them. Her hands move to the back of his neck and pulled his mouth closer; it was clear she wanted this kiss as badly as he did. Taking the kiss deeper, wrapped in each other's arms under nothing but the light of the moon, Chase had never felt anything so right.

In that moment, all doubt disappeared and he had never been more certain—Emma Woods was meant for him.

CHAPTER 12

*E*mma flipped over in bed to get a view of the clock. 1:02 a.m. How long was she going to lie wide awake, replaying the kiss with Chase over in her mind? At the foot of the bed, she could hear Zeke's gentle snore. *At least someone can sleep.*

She moved her fingers to her lips and held them there, unable to shake the feeling of Chase's mouth on hers. The way the scent of his cologne had ignited her passion for him when he pulled her close, the way his strong arms felt so safe wrapped around her body, the way his lips felt so soft, and the way they had tasted so good—it was all filling her with a giddy schoolgirl energy, as if it was her first kiss ever.

But it hadn't been her first kiss ever. It was, however, the first kiss that ever made her feel like this. Something about it just felt so ... *right.* There was an undeniable chemistry between them when their lips touched. Not only did the kiss feel like nothing she'd ever experienced, but it had intensified every feeling she had for Chase times a million. There was no doubt in her mind they belonged together now. The only question was, why had they waited so long?

But had Chase felt it, too? The curiosity of what he was feeling and thinking was getting the best of her. She sat up and looked at the clock again. 1:04 a.m. Grabbing her cell phone off the nightstand, she typed out a text:

You awake?

Nothing.

Of course, he was sleeping. Why would he be awake at this hour after he'd worked hard on the house all day? He was probably exhausted, and she was being foolish. She just hoped her invasive late night text hadn't woken him.

Her phone buzzed in her hand and the screen lit up, sending a jolt of excitement through Emma's system as she read the screen.

Can't sleep. I was gonna ask you the same.

Her heart pounded in her chest. She hesitated for a moment, trying to think of what to say now that she was certain he was just as hot and bothered by their kiss as she was.

What's on your mind? She finally typed out and sent the text before she could delete it.

A long pause from Chase had her holding her phone in one hand, chewing at a cuticle on the other.

You. Your lips. That kiss.

Reading Chase's words on the screen sent a ripple of tingling sensations through her body. To think he was lying in bed, only a couple hundred yards away, replaying their kiss over in his mind, unable to sleep just like she was? What would she send in response to that?

Me too.

Nothing too clever, but at least now he knew she was on the same page.

Any regrets?

Not a single one.

Good. Does that mean you're ready to stop fighting this?

Fighting what?

This undeniable connection between us.

I stopped fighting it at the beach, remember?

Oh, I remember. So, does that mean we can give this a try?

You and me?

Yes, you and me.

I'm ready to try if you are.

Then it's official?

It's official.

A series of kissy face emojis appeared on her screen before Chase's next text.

See you in the morning, Em.

Good night, Chase.

Knowing that her and Chase were finally going to give their relationship a try, Emma was finally able to lie back down and doze off, visions of Chase's lips alive in her dreams.

Chase made his way over to the main house the next morning, excited to see Emma. He couldn't wait to plant a kiss on her lips and have coffee with her on the front porch. He opened the back door and was immediately greeted by a very excited black Lab with a wet tongue.

"Hey, boy. Where's your mom?" He'd developed quite the relationship with Zeke being in the house together all week. He was sure Zeke could understand all of their conversations, even if he couldn't respond.

Chase made his way to the kitchen to put on the coffee, and

to his dismay, found a note sitting in front of the coffee pot instead.

Had to go in early today. I'm doing all the baking for the party.

Don't forget, we have to be at the resort by 6. Can't wait to see you.

~Em

How could he forget? He'd been looking forward to Hunter and Rylee's engagement party all week. His heart plummeted at the thought of having to wait until this evening to see Emma. He'd just have to keep himself busy today to pass the time. He'd figured there was no better time than now to get started on the upstairs.

Emma arrived at NovelTea and was pleased to find Rose had come in early to help her. "Good morning, Rose. You're here early," Emma said, pulling an apron over her head and tying it around her waist.

"I know you have a big day. I'm not going to leave you to do all this baking alone." Rose looked up and smiled before going back to the dough she was kneading. Then Rose dropped the dough and headed over to Emma and stopped right in front of her. "I see I was right," she said with a wink.

"Right about what?" Emma asked, confusion clouding her thoughts.

"I told you that man was crazy about you."

Emma cocked a hand on her hip and looked up from the pan she was prepping. "What makes you think that?"

"Well, am I wrong?"

A smile dug its way into Emma's cheeks. She tried to

control it, but there was no denying. She was dying to tell someone about Chase, and Rose wouldn't judge. Rose was the best person to talk to about this. "You were so right, Rose," Emma beamed.

"I'm glad to hear it. You deserve happiness, Emma. I haven't seen you this happy about a man … well, ever."

"Aaron isn't going to like it."

"Ah, Aaron who?" Rose teased, swatting at the air with her hand. "Aaron was never for you. He was a companion and someone you passed time with. You never looked at him the way you do this one. This Chase is your once-in-a-lifetime love, and let me tell you, you only get one of those. Best not let him slip away," Rose warned with a pitched brow.

Was that true? People only got one great love in their lifetime? It sure seemed like it to Emma. Nobody had ever made her feel the way Chase did. And the way they were together, it was like they were made for each other. She wasn't sure why she had fought it for so long, but there was no denying it now.

Emma was head over heels in love with Chase Knox.

Time seemed to stand still for Emma. Once she'd gotten all the baking done for the party and Shane had picked it up, she was left with the afternoon lull they always had mid-day at Novel-Tea. She couldn't have been happier when the clock struck five, and it was time to close up and get home to Chase.

Walking into Hemlock House, she expected Zeke to greet her, but there was no sign of him. He must be out back in the guesthouse with Chase. She made her way to the kitchen and stopped short in the doorway, the sight before her causing her heart to skip a beat.

The most beautiful arrangement of white and red roses greeted her from the butcher's block—at least two dozen. Poking out of it, she could see a little white card. She walked over, took a moment to lean down and smell one of the white roses, and then pulled the card from the envelope.

White for our friendship, and red for our love. May both last forever.

~Chase

Emma's heart melted at the sight of the words. Who knew Chase had a romantic side to him? With the giddiness of a young girl, she made her way upstairs to get ready for the party.

She showered and then chose a blue A-line dress—Chase's favorite color—and nude peep-toe heels. She decided she'd wear her hair down tonight, allowing her long, wavy locks to cascade down her back and around her shoulders. She applied a hint of makeup and grabbed a nude clutch to match her shoes.

It had been a long time since she'd gotten ready with the thought of a man in mind. Usually, she just grabbed anything, but now she really wanted to look nice for Chase. And when she rounded the corner at the top of the stairs, she could see Chase standing at the bottom waiting for her, looking rather dapper himself.

Her pulse quickened with each step on her way to meet him, and when she got to the bottom step, he made his way over and put his arm around her waist, pulling her into him for a light peck to the lips before adding, "Wow. You look stunning, Em."

"You don't look too bad yourself, Mr. Knox," she said with a smile. "Thank you so much for the flowers; they're beautiful."

"Not as beautiful as you." He held out his arm for hers. "Shall we?"

They headed out the front door and around the side to Emma's truck, ready to make their first public appearance as a couple.

CHAPTER 13

*W*alking onto the veranda at Arbor Shores Resort with Emma by his side was surreal. It was only a few minutes past six, but most of the guests were already mingling, and it seemed like almost everyone stopped and turned in their direction when they made their appearance hand in hand. Chase gave Emma's hand a reassuring squeeze and straightened his back, ready to show off their new relationship to family and friends.

Hunter and Rylee made their way over to greet them. "Look at you two. If I didn't know better, I'd think you were a couple," Rylee observed, leaning in to take turns kissing each of them on the cheek.

Emma and Chase exchanged glances and smiled before turning their attention back to Hunter and Rylee.

Hunter placed a hand on Chase's shoulder. "I'm glad you could be here. It means a lot to me to have two of my brothers here tonight."

"I'm glad to be here, too. Congratulations on the engagement. Hey, where do we put the gifts?" Chase asked, nodding to the present he was carrying under his left arm.

"Aww, you shouldn't have," Hunter teased. "Come with me."

"I'll be back," Chase leaned in to plant a light kiss to Emma's forehead before following Hunter across the patio to the gift table.

Once Chase set down the gift, he noticed Hunter was looking at him with a suspicious grin. "Okay, spill it."

"Spill what?" Chase played dumb, but he had a feeling he knew what his brother was hinting toward.

"What's going on with you and Emma?"

"Is it that obvious?"

"It's that obvious." Hunter shook his head and laughed.

"Man, I'm crazy about that girl. There's no denying it."

"Well, everyone already knew that, Chase. You've always been crazy about her. The question is, have you two decided to stop playing the 'just friends' act and give in to your affection for one another?"

"Actually, yeah, we have. It just kind of happened." Chase let out a long breath and shoved his hands into his pockets. It felt good to say it out loud.

"Well, it's about time." Hunter slapped Chase on the back. "I'm happy for you."

"It's about time for what?" Shane asked, joining his brothers.

"Chase and Emma have finally stopped pretending they aren't madly in love with each other."

"Really? It *is* about time," Shane teased. "Seriously though, that's awesome, bro. Emma's a great girl and you both deserve happiness. I hope this means you'll be sticking around for a while?"

"That's the plan. We're going to reopen Hemlock House together. As business partners."

Hunter's brow shot up. "Really? Mixing business with pleasure?" Chase suspected Hunter might not think it was a good idea. He was the business-savvy one of the brothers.

"Shane and Avery do it, and look at this place," Chase said, holding his arms up and motioning around the resort.

"Yes, Shane and Avery have really turned this place around. Just be careful is all I'm saying. You'll need a formal agreement."

"Well, that's the thing. She's having Aaron Reynolds draw up the paperwork. I'm not crazy about that." Chase rubbed at the back of his neck.

"Well, I don't trust that guy. He's only going to have Emma's interests in mind. Before you sign anything, make sure you bring it to me to look over. I can have my attorney look over it as well."

Chase wasn't sure what was causing Hunter's hesitation, but it was a nice offer and reassuring to know he had his brother in his corner. Before he could respond, Avery came over and ushered everyone to their seats, indicating it was time for dinner.

Chase pulled Emma's chair out for her, and she smiled up at him appreciatively. It was a beautiful evening for dinner on the veranda, and the setting was perfect. Chase hadn't been to the resort since he was a teenager, but it was just as nice as he remembered, if not more. They were on the backside of the massive, log cabin-style main lodge, high atop a hill overlooking Lake Michigan. The sun was beginning to set into the lake, and the sky was a medley of orange and magenta beyond the evergreens that dotted the shoreline. Above them, small white lights hung across the patio, matching the crisp white linens adorning each table, while a jazz band played a light tune in the corner.

They had dinner followed by dessert, and then the band picked up the beat as everyone got up to mingle with an after-dinner drink. Hunter took the microphone and told the story of how he'd proposed to Rylee on his yacht last month, but Chase wasn't sure what all he had said. He'd been too fixated on Emma to hear his brother's words. He just knew Hunter was madly in love with Rylee, and Chase couldn't have been happier for them.

As they all stood, Carter and Valerie made their way over. Carter was scanning Chase and Emma as they approached, and Chase could tell he was taking notice of Emma's arm looped through his.

"I was hoping we'd get a chance to talk with you two before we left. I don't know why they had us seated across the veranda," Valerie said, drawing near to Emma and Chase.

Chase was proud to have Emma on his arm, and he didn't plan to let her go just because his father was eyeing the two of them. He couldn't tell if that was approval on his father's stoic face or not. Only time would tell.

"Nice to see you again, Valerie, Carter," Emma said, addressing each of them.

"Hi, Dad. Hey, Valerie," Chase said, following suit.

"Emma, son," Carter said and nodded, taking a sip of his scotch and looking out over the horizon.

"We'd love it if you two could join us for dinner. This week?" Valerie asked.

Chase looked to Emma and waited for her to respond.

"We'd love that," Emma told them with a polite smile.

"Have you given any more thought to sticking around here?" Carter asked, looking Chase square in the eye now.

"Yes, I have. I've decided to stay in Arbor Shores. We're going to reopen Hemlock House together," Chase admitted. He sucked in a breath and awaited his father's reaction, hoping to gain his approval.

"Is that so?" Carter asked, looking back and forth between the two of them.

"Oh, I'm so pleased to hear that," Valerie beamed. "Hemlock House was always so lovely, and of course, we're glad to have you back for good, Chase." Chase wasn't sure why Valerie was being so nice to him. He didn't know her all that much, but she hadn't seemed to care for him during the short time they'd lived together in the Knox Estate before Chase had been kicked out. Maybe time had changed her. It had seemed to change his father.

"Yes, we'll have dinner and discuss the details. Tomorrow night. Yacht club." Carter told them. It was more of a demand than a question. Chase knew the businessman side of his father wasn't going to let one of his sons go into business without overseeing it. A part of him appreciated that his father cared at all, but another part of him wanted to do it on his own. Still, Chase didn't trust Aaron, and the fact that both Hunter and Carter were willing to oversee the details was reassuring. He needed someone on his side, and he didn't have an attorney of his own like Emma had.

Chase and Emma agreed to dinner at the yacht club at seven the following evening, and Valerie and Carter said their goodbyes, leaving Chase alone with Emma on the corner of the veranda. The sun had fully set now, and the moon was shining down on the lake. Chase noticed Emma take in a yawn.

"Ready to get out of here?" he asked.

"It's just been a long day. I'm ready to get home and into my pajamas." Emma glanced at her watch.

"Come on. I'll get you home so you can get to bed." He held out his hand for her.

Emma laughed and took his hand. "I didn't say I was ready for bed. I was hoping we could have another movie night." She flashed him a flirtatious grin. Chase's pulse quickened at the thought of a night on the couch with Emma.

"There's nothing I'd rather do than cuddle with you and Zeke and watch a movie," he told her as he took her by the hand. They made their way over to the crew to say their goodbyes.

As they left the party, Chase was feeling better than ever. He and Emma had made their newfound relationship public, he'd gotten what he'd take as an approval from his father for the first time in his life, and he had Emma by his side.

There was nothing that could bring him down from this high. For the first time in his life, Chase felt like he was exactly where he was meant to be, and that felt good.

Back at Hemlock House, Chase and Emma went their respective ways to change out of their evening attire and into loungewear before meeting back in the kitchen to make popcorn and then retiring to the parlor to watch a movie. They decided on a romantic comedy—Emma's pick.

Cuddled up on the couch with Zeke at their feet, Emma couldn't be any more content. It had been a long time since she'd had someone to snuggle with, and she couldn't remember the last time she'd even had company over before Chase. This was something she had never done with Aaron. He always wanted to be out on the town socializing and making appearances, whereas Emma was more of a homebody. She'd rather be home watching a movie with Chase than anywhere else in the world right now. She just hoped this lifestyle would be enough to keep him content, because he had an itch to travel and see the world. Would she be enough to keep him here? The last thing she wanted to do was open a business together and then have him take off again.

On second thought, she trusted him. He said he was staying, and he seemed to be into her, so it was time to move forward with their plan. No looking back, no second-guessing. All she needed was for Aaron to finalize their agreement, and they would be able to open for business in the next week or so. Before long, they'd be bringing in income, and she'd be able to hire an extra employee to help out at NovelTea, which meant more time with Chase.

With Chase's arm around her, she nuzzled up next to him and draped her legs over his. The smell of his cologne still lingered ever so slightly, igniting her desire to kiss him. He held her right hand, and caressed her palm softly with his thumb, a tiny gesture that was causing monumental things to happen inside her. She'd been longing for another kiss since her lips parted from his on the beach, and being this close to Chase was making it hard for her to concentrate on the movie.

She lifted her head up and looked at him, her face only inches from his. He looked down at her, a knowing look in his eyes. She didn't have to say what she wanted. He leaned forward and placed his lips on hers, kissing her ever so gently at first. Turning his body toward her, he wrapped his arms around her tightly and pulled her onto his lap in one suave move.

They spent the rest of the evening tangled on the couch, making out like a couple of teenagers. Neither of them noticing when the movie came to an end.

The next morning, Emma awoke to the smell of sausage wafting through the air. That meant Chase must've been cooking her breakfast, and the fact that Zeke was nowhere to be found confirmed her suspicions.

After a hot shower, she was getting ready to head downstairs when she noticed her phone light up on her nightstand.

A text from Aaron.

A knot formed in her throat. Eventually, she would need to have a conversation with him about her and Chase, but now was not the time. Not that she owed him an explanation. He wasn't her boyfriend and she was not by any means committed to him. But she had spent time with him, and he cared about her, so out of respect for his feelings, she owed it to him to tell him about Chase herself before he found out through someone else.

She decided that on Monday when she went back to his office to get the paperwork, she would tell him then. In person. For now, she'd better check his text in case he was working on the agreement and had a question about Hemlock House.

She clicked his name on the screen to open the text.

Dinner tonight?

She blew out a sigh and contemplated her response.

I can't tonight, sorry.

A long pause caused her to set the phone back on the nightstand, but before she walked away, it lit up again.

Plans with Chase?

Something about his question made her blood boil. He had no right to ask her these types of questions. It was none of his business, and he was acting jealous—a huge turn off for her.

She didn't feel like she needed to lie; she had no reason to. She picked up the phone to respond.

Having dinner with the Knoxes at the yacht club tonight. See you tomorrow.

She tossed the phone back on her nightstand and made her way downstairs. She didn't want to keep Chase waiting, and she was craving not only his cooking but his lips, too.

Just as she expected, she found Chase at the stove with Zeke loyally by his side. *Traitor.* But she had to smile. She loved seeing Zeke's affection for Chase. He'd never taken to Aaron for some reason, and that never set right with her. She cleared her throat.

Chase turned, an instant smile lighting up his face. "Good morning."

"You know, you're going to have to stop spoiling me like this. I might just get used to it," she told him, making her way over to the stove and pecking him on the lips to distract him while stealing a slice of sausage.

"Well, get used to it because I'm not going anywhere."

That was all she needed to hear. Elation engulfed her, and this sexy man in her kitchen was all to blame.

Chase grabbed a plate from the cupboard and shimmied the omelet from the pan onto its surface, handing it to Emma. He followed her into the dining room with his plate and took a seat across from her.

"Mmm, this is delicious," she moaned, taking a bite of her omelet. "I love having you here, by the way. In case I haven't told you."

Chase laughed. "Because I cook for you?"

"No!" She shot him her best how-dare-you glare, then added, "Well, okay, your cooking is a bonus. But really, I love waking up and having you here and knowing that you're never too far away."

"Well, I love being here," he said when he finished chewing his bite. "I love being with *you*."

She put down her fork and took a deep breath before asking the question nibbling at her mind. "Chase, promise me you're not going to leave me again."

"Emma, we've been over this." He reached across the table and placed his hand on top of hers.

"I just need you to tell me one more time before we sign the papers."

Chase got up and made his way around the table, holding out his hand to her. She looked at his hand for a moment, then placed hers in his as he helped her to her feet before pulling her in for a hug.

"You have to trust me, or this is never going to work," he whispered in her ear.

"I trust you. I just don't want to lose you. And I don't want to reopen Hemlock House if there is any chance you are going to leave again."

Chase stepped back and cupped her face gently with both hands, looking deep into her eyes. "Em, I love you. Did you know that?"

"You do?"

"Of course, I do. And that means I'm not going anywhere. Ever. You're the only one in the world for me. And there's nothing I'd rather do than grow old in this big ole house with you."

His words stole the breath from her lungs, so she shook her head yes to indicate that she believed him, relief rippling through her body.

"Is that it?" he asked.

"What do you mean?"

"I told you I love you. Don't you have anything else to say?" he teased, but she could tell he was waiting for her response.

A smile spread across her face. "Of course. I love you, too."

CHAPTER 14

*H*earing Emma's words caused Chase's heart to swell with pride. Finally, he'd put any lingering hesitations she had to rest, and he had the love of his dream girl.

They finished breakfast and then headed into the city to get the new bedding for the rooms. That was the last of the final touches that needed to be made before they could reopen Hemlock House. Now, all they needed to do was finalize their agreement; Emma was meeting with Aaron tomorrow to get the paperwork.

Of course, Chase would have Hunter look over the paperwork as well, just to make sure Aaron hadn't pulled anything, but then he planned to sign it, and as long as all their permits were in place, they would be ready to open doors on their B&B by the following weekend. But there was still a thought niggling at Chase's brain. He wasn't exactly sure how building permits worked, but what if Aaron had to do a background check to secure the licensing and permits they needed? If Emma ever found out about his past and what he'd been hiding, surely she'd never want to go into business with him. A wave of guilt washed over him. Didn't she have a right to know anyway? He couldn't carry this secret any longer. Tomorrow night, before they sat down to sign the papers, he would tell her the truth. He'd made up his mind.

Problem was, they'd already made plans for a grand opening party, yet they hadn't begun accepting reservations just yet. Mainly because they'd spent so much on renovations, and there wasn't much left for website development or the online reservation system they needed. In the meantime, they'd have to rely on word of mouth and the good old fashioned phone system until they could afford a proper reservation system. Then, they could begin advertising.

Now, it was time to meet Carter and Valerie for dinner, and although things were going well between him and his father, the thought of sitting through an entire meal while being drilled by Carter about their business plan had his stomach in knots. Chase was just happy to have Emma by his side. Somehow, she made everyday life easier. Actually, she made *everything* easier.

Pulling into the Arbor Shores Yacht Club in Emma's old pickup truck, Chase decided to skip valet and self-park. Not that they had any reason to be ashamed, but it was clear he didn't belong in his father's world and he didn't need another reminder how "less than" he was from Carter Knox.

Chase held out his arm to Emma, and she looped hers through his as he escorted her inside. The hostess informed them that Carter and Valerie were already seated in the lounge, and they followed her to a corner table—his father's self-proclaimed table for as far back as Chase could remember. Growing up, his father frequented the yacht club several nights per week, and they had dinner there as a family on most

Sundays before their parents had divorced. Once Valerie came into the picture, they stopped doing things as a family altogether.

Approaching the table, Valerie stood to greet them, but Carter stayed seated. He was already sipping his scotch, and something about that caused a nervous energy to charge through Chase's system. His father was walking a fine line each time he drank the stuff, and Chase didn't ever want to see him cross that line again. Hopefully they were beyond those days—he prayed he'd never have to experience the wrath of his father's temper again.

After the server came over and took their drink order, Valerie started, "So, what are your plans for Hemlock House? When will you reopen?"

"Chase has really outdone himself. He spent the entire week fixing up the place. We'd like to open next weekend," Emma said.

"That soon?" Carter asked, leaning back in his chair, his glass of scotch glued to his hand.

"Yeah, it's ready to go." Chase looked at Emma and smiled. She met his smile with her own.

"What's the arrangement between the two of you? Do you think you'll be married?" Valerie asked.

Chase nearly choked on the sip of water he had just taken. Even though the thought of having Emma for his wife was something that he could get used to, he'd never expected anyone to ask that question so soon. They'd only officially been together a week. How would he answer?

"Uh, we are entering as official business partners." Chase decided to ignore the question altogether, and wondered if his answer was hurtful to Emma or a relief.

"You realize the risks involved in going into business

together while dating. What if it doesn't work out? What if you split up?" Carter had a condescending tone that was causing a fire to ignite inside Chase.

"That's not going to happen." Chase was quick to respond. "And if it did—*hypothetically*—then we'd remain friends. We'd still be able to be business partners."

"Well, you need to be sure to address that in the agreement." Carter leaned forward and set his scotch down, but not before taking another sip.

"It will be addressed," Emma spoke up to reassure him, her admission a shock to Chase. That was essentially what the agreement was for, but thinking of her discussing that with Aaron outside of Chase's presence didn't sit well with him.

The server delivered a charcuterie board, and the conversation finally shifted—a relief to Chase. He was already feeling hot around the collar with the questions being fired at them, and he just wished he could fast forward through this evening and be back at Hemlock House, alone with Emma.

By the time they were finished with the main course, Chase was feeling a bit more relaxed. Emma was winning over Valerie with talks about how her parents had run Hemlock House and what they planned to keep the same and what all they planned to do differently. His father was quiet most of the time, but Chase knew he was taking it all in.

When the server delivered a round of dessert and coffee to the table, Carter pushed his to the side and held up his empty glass, indicating that he wanted another scotch. Chase had counted three, so this would be number four, and if memory served, that was the tipping point. Chase knew it was time for he and Emma to make their exit.

"Well, we should probably get going soon. Emma has to be up early in the morning to open NovelTea."

"Nonsense, you just got your dessert," Carter said, shooting Chase a look—one that Chase still found intimidating and that still managed to make him feel small, even after all this time.

"Carter, dear, do you want to tell them what we discussed on the way over?" Valerie gave him a pointed look. Chase sucked in a deep breath and held it. There was no telling what was about to come out of his father's mouth.

"Ah, yes," Carter began and sat up straight in his chair for the first time all night. Clasping his hands in front of him on the table, he said, "Knox Enterprises would like to offer Hemlock House a business development grant. Just a small chunk of money to get you two started and off on the right foot."

This time, Chase did begin to choke. Had he heard his father right? He wanted to give them funding for their business? As much as they could use it, there was no way Chase was accepting a handout from his father. This was the first business he'd ever started, and he wouldn't allow his father to have a hand in it. Chase had something to prove, and it was important to him that he and Emma did this on their own.

He glanced over at Emma, and although she wasn't one to take handouts, she was looking at Chase with hopeful eyes. A grant would offer them the money for a website and social media advertising campaign that would get the word out downstate to the travelers that liked to travel north on the weekends. It would also allow Emma to hire someone for NovelTea sooner rather than later so she could pitch in and help Chase at Hemlock House.

"That's a kind offer, thank you, but we can do this on our own," Chase said.

"Chase, dear, you should take the grant." Valerie leaned

over and placed her hand on his. "Knox Enterprises is known for offering funding to small businesses in town. It could really help you get the B&B off the ground quickly."

"Thank you for the generous offer, Carter," Emma spoke up. "We'll discuss it."

Chase could tell she wanted to entertain the idea, and even though he had no plan of accepting the grant, it wouldn't be fair not to hear her out. They were partners, after all, and she deserved an opinion in the matter.

"Thank you for the offer. We'll discuss it tonight," Chase told his father.

If someone had told him two weeks ago that he'd be in this position, he never would have believed them. Here he was, sitting at a table across from his father who was offering to fund his new business startup, with his dream girl and business partner on his right. Everything was going so well, he almost felt as if he was dreaming. For a moment, he thought nothing could bring him down. That is, until he caught a glimpse of Aaron Reynolds out of the corner of his eye, making his way toward their table, a manila envelope in his hand. Was it their agreement? Why couldn't he wait until tomorrow like he and Emma had planned? Chase didn't want his father seeing the agreement before he had a chance to look it over. His pulse began to quicken as Aaron drew near.

"Good evening, Carter, Valerie." Aaron addressed the Knoxes as he approached the table.

Chase's jaw clenched. Why was Aaron even here? Obviously, he was a member or he wouldn't be able to get in. But how had he known they'd be there tonight?

"Well, good evening, Aaron," Carter said. "Care to join us?"

"No, thank you. I don't want to interrupt. This won't take

long." Aaron fired a glare at Chase, and Chase's fists instinctively balled at his sides below the table as he watched Aaron pull paperwork from the manila envelope and toss it on the center of the table.

Chase's heart slammed against his chest when his eyes fell on the rap sheet before him. There it was, Chase's mugshot staring back at him, and the charges that had been filed against him that fateful night in New York. A night that was beyond his control. A night he'd hoped to keep hidden.

"I'm afraid I won't be able to move forward with creating your agreement, Emma," Aaron started. "It appears your new business partner here has been locked up for the past six months for grand theft. As the head of the Arbor Shores tourism board, I think I speak on behalf of the committee when I say we don't want a convicted felon opening a B&B in Arbor Shores. Especially one who steals."

All eyes darted to Chase. Carter picked up the paperwork, and the air was sucked out of Chase's lungs as he watched his father peruse his criminal record.

"Is this true, Chase?" Emma asked, the look of disappointment on her face was like a knife to his chest.

Chase couldn't breathe, much less respond. How would he ever make them understand?

"I'll leave you four alone with that. It looks like you have a lot to discuss." Aaron turned and headed back to the bar.

Carter slammed his fists on the table, causing the silverware to jump and the coffee to splash out of the cups and onto the white linen. "Out of the country, huh, Chase?"

Chase's heart plummeted. He was called out on the only lie he'd ever told. He couldn't look at Emma. He could feel her stare boring into him, along with everyone else's in the room, and he just wanted nothing more than to disappear.

"It's not what it looks like. I can explain," Chase started, a mixture of panic and anger taking over him.

Carter rose to his feet. "I don't need you to explain. It's all right here in black and white." Carter shook the papers in the air, causing quite the scene for the members around them. The whole room went silent, and Chase could see Aaron gloating from his barstool across the room.

"I'm telling you—" Chase started, but he was quickly cut off by his father's scotch-induced rage.

"You good-for-nothing, sorry excuse for a son. Get out of here and get out of my life! I don't raise thieves, and I don't raise felons," Carter spat through gritted teeth.

Chase rose from the table, throwing the fork down that he'd been gripping, causing a clanging sound to ripple through the room. He pushed his way past servers who'd stopped what they were doing to watch the scene unfold, and made his way toward the door, leaving Emma, Valerie and Carter at the table. He wanted as far away from his father as possible.

Humiliation flooded through him and he couldn't get away fast enough. He'd never felt overcome by such embarrassment in all his life. Right now, he just wanted to get back to Hemlock House, pack his bags and get out of town. He was sure Emma wouldn't want anything to do with him, and there was no way they could move forward with their business now. He'd heard Aaron; nobody wanted a convicted felon opening a business in town. Having his name tied to the business would ruin Hemlock House for Emma. The best thing to do would be to get out of her life once and for all.

He began running toward the road. He'd run the two miles back to town and get his stuff and be gone. His only hope was that he'd get out before he saw her.

He never wanted to have to face Emma again.

Emma stood, ready to head to the door and run after Chase. "I'm sorry about this, Mr. and Mrs. Knox. I had no idea." She grabbed her purse off the back of the chair and excused herself from the table. "Thank you for dinner."

Emma was seething inside, partly because Chase had lied to her, but more so at Aaron for airing Chase's dirty laundry publicly in an attempt to ruin his reputation. Aaron not only destroyed any chance for them to reopen Hemlock House, but he'd exposed Chase at the yacht club of all places, which meant all of Arbor Shores would know by morning. The news could potentially put NovelTea's reputation in jeopardy as well.

As soon as she made it to the front door of the yacht club, she began running toward her truck. She had to find Chase. As mad as she was at him, she didn't want him walking home, and Pine Ridge Way was a dangerous road with many twists and turns and no sidewalks to keep him out of harm's way.

Emma took three quick lunges forward before feeling the heel of her pump lodge into something, causing her body to catapult through the air and land on all fours on the rough asphalt parking lot beyond the sidewalk.

"Emma!" Aaron yelled as he came out the door behind her, making his way toward her.

She was on her hands and knees, one shoe on, and when she managed to turn her head around, she noticed her right heel had gotten stuck between the cracks in the sidewalk. A sharp pain from her right ankle shot up her leg when she tried to put pressure on it to get up. "Ow!" she exclaimed, surrendering to the pavement and putting her foot back out behind her.

Aaron made his way to her side and picked her up, placing her down on the weight of her left foot while she held the other in the air like a wounded bird. He draped her arm over his shoulder as a crutch.

"Don't touch me," she hissed when she noticed it was Aaron who had helped her up.

"Emma, are you okay?" he asked, ignoring her question.

"I'm fine. I have to go. I have to get to Chase," she told him as she attempted once again to put weight on her right foot. But the shooting pain traveling up her leg told her something was wrong. She just prayed it wasn't broken.

"You're not fine, Emma. Something is wrong with your foot. I'm taking you to the hospital," Aaron demanded, motioning for the valet to bring his car around.

"I'm not going anywhere with you after what you just did in there."

"Well, you certainly can't drive with your right foot the way it is. And it looks like your thief of a boyfriend left you. You're coming with me to the hospital."

She hated to get in the car with Aaron, but he was right. She couldn't drive with her right foot. She couldn't even move it. Right now, like it or not, she was at his mercy. She'd have to deal with this first and then talk to Chase when she got home.

It took Chase twenty-five minutes to jog back to town from the yacht club. Even though he wasn't ready to face her, every time he heard a car coming from behind him, he expected it to be her. Yet, none of the four cars that passed him were hers. Perhaps, somehow, she'd passed him without him noticing?

But when he rounded the corner to Main Street and got a

clear view of the empty driveway at Hemlock House, his heart sank. Things were definitely over between them. Emma hadn't come after him, which meant she was either still at the yacht club discussing his business with the Knoxes, or worse, she had left with Aaron. That thought twisted at his heart.

He made his way inside the guesthouse and grabbed his duffel bag from the closet, pulling clothes from their hangers and stuffing them into the bag along with the rest of his belongings. When he'd finally packed what little he owned, he walked outside and paused. Should he go inside the main house to say goodbye to Zeke? Nah, that would be too painful. He'd grown attached to that dog. It would be better just to leave without having to see him again.

Same with Emma. He would've liked the opportunity to explain himself. But he was too embarrassed to see her, and plus, the fact that she'd stayed at the yacht club told him everything he needed to know about where they now stood. He wasn't good enough for her, so it was only natural she would gravitate back to Aaron. What was Chase thinking to believe he could ever get a girl like Emma? The Chase she thought she was in love with turned out to be a liar and a felon. That thought punched at his heart as he straddled his bike and powered up the engine. The worst part was he'd planned to come clean with her tomorrow night. But Aaron had gotten to her before he had the chance, so she'd never believe Chase had intended to tell her the truth.

Squealing his tires as he peeled out of the driveway, he took Main Street to Pine Ridge Way and headed south of town, ready to leave Arbor Shores once and for all.

But first, he had one last stop to make.

CHAPTER 15

Chase paused in front of Hunter's front door. Should he knock? He wondered if his brother would even believe his side of the story. Had his father already gotten to him and told Hunter that Chase was a lying thief? It was possible, but still, he wanted to say goodbye in person, at least to one of his brothers, and he didn't know where Shane lived. Surely, Hunter would be home at 10 p.m. on a Sunday, and he was driving by on his way out of town anyway.

Chase rang the bell and waited. After a long pause, he saw an interior light flip on through the window and heard Hunter call out from beyond the door, "Coming."

The large front door swung open and a look of confusion spread across his brother's face. "Chase, what are you doing here? Is everything okay?" Hunter moved to the side and allowed Chase to enter. That was a good sign. Apparently, news of Chase's past hadn't started to spread just yet.

"I wanted to stop and say goodbye in person," Chase said, taking a look around, relieved that Hunter appeared to be alone.

"Goodbye? What are you talking about?" Hunter half laughed, as if in disbelief.

"Haven't you heard?"

"Uh-oh, this doesn't sound good. Let me grab us a beer. I'll meet you on the back patio."

Chase made his way out through the wall of glass that made up the backside of Hunter's home, to be welcomed by a cool, freshwater breeze coming off the lake. It was dark now, so he couldn't see the water. He could only hear the gentle sound of waves lapping the shore, soothing him as he took a seat on a lounge chair and waited for Hunter to join him.

"What's going on?" Hunter asked, appearing from behind him and handing him a beer.

"So much, Hunter. I don't even know where to begin." Chase looked over at his brother and took a long pull off his beer before setting it down next to him. He leaned forward and put his elbows on his knees and put his head in his hands.

"The beginning," Hunter told him, setting his own beer down and shifting his body to face Chase.

"Okay," Chase agreed. After a long pause to find his words, he started, "Before I came back to Arbor Shores, I wasn't actually out of the country."

"Okay." Hunter didn't sound pleased at Chase's admission, but at least he was giving him space to explain, and Chase could appreciate that.

"I was in New York City, and I was working as a bodyguard for a high-profile teenage actor."

"Why would you have to lie about that?"

He sat back in the chair and looked over at his brother. "You said to start at the beginning. I'm getting there."

"Ah, okay then. Go on."

"I don't want to say who he was, but he had a major film

release last year, and the paparazzi were following him every-where. This was the film that was supposed to put him on the map. The kid had a lot going for him, but he had been in and out of trouble in the past, so his parents hired me not only to protect him, but to keep him in line."

"Keep going."

"Well, he had a bit of a shoplifting problem, one that I didn't know about until he got caught. He was so good at it that I never even noticed, and I was the one watching over him." Chase paused and took a drink. "Until we were shopping one Sunday. I was driving, and we were involved in an acci-dent due to the paparazzi chasing us. The retailers had managed to keep the photogs out of the store so we could shop, but as soon as we got in the car, they were relentless in trying to snap photos of him. I was watching them in my rearview mirror when I plowed into the car in front of us."

"So, you somehow got blamed for the stolen goods, I take it?"

"Exactly. As soon as the accident happened, he started pulling stuff off his body and shoving it under my driver's seat. He was sitting in the back seat, behind me." Chase got up and began to pace the deck. "When the police arrived, they were examining the vehicles and conducting an investigation. They saw something sticking out from under my seat and that's how they found all of it. They immediately thought it was mine."

"Why didn't you tell on the kid?"

"I don't know, man. Looking back, because I took my job very seriously. I was hired to protect him, and to me that meant at all costs. Plus, I had grown close to him—I saw a lot of myself in him, ya know? I didn't want him to ruin his life over a stupid mistake."

"Sounds like you also made a stupid mistake by not telling the police. What'd you get charged with?"

"I ended up charged with grand theft because he had taken jewelry. Lots of it."

"Are you out on parole then? How were you able to leave the state?"

"No parole. The judge only sentenced me to six months because I didn't have any priors. I served my time."

"So, that's why we couldn't get ahold of you when Dad had his heart attack," Hunter said.

"I came as soon as I was released and found out about Dad. But you have to understand, I was ashamed, and I wasn't prepared to come home and tell everyone I was fresh out of the pen."

"So, you made up a story about Costa Rica?"

"Well, yes and no. The story about Costa Rica is true. Except that happened three years ago. I fibbed about the timeline."

A long pause from his brother was causing Chase's brow to moisten.

"I understand," Hunter finally said quietly, looking straight ahead out into the dark abyss before them.

"Anyway, Emma and I were having dinner with Dad and Valerie tonight when Aaron Reynolds decided to take it upon himself to reveal my past to the entire yacht club. Long story short, Emma wants nothing to do with me, and we can't open the B&B now since I have a felony conviction."

"Well, let's just think about this for the moment." Hunter rose to his feet and started pacing himself. After a minute or two, he finally said, "You didn't actually do it, so therefore, you were wrongfully accused."

"Yes."

"So, you were convicted of a crime you didn't actually commit."

"Technically, yes."

"Did you plead guilty?"

"No, I pled not guilty. I said it wasn't mine, because that was the truth. I just never ratted on the kid."

"Ah-ha!" Hunter's face lit up.

"What are you so excited about?" Chase asked.

"You never pled guilty. So, you did time for a crime you never committed. We can get you recovered of these charges, Chase. We just have to prove your innocence."

"No, that kid is never gonna fess up. He's a famous actor now. He's not going to ruin his career for me. I could never get him to admit to it at this point."

"You wouldn't have to. That's what lawyers are for, and I happen to have the best lawyers money can buy."

"What are you saying?" Chase had a glimmer of hope for the first time since Aaron had crushed his world.

"I'm saying that if you would've had decent attorneys at the time, you may not have been convicted at all. Likely, you couldn't afford them at the time, but I can, and I'm willing to do that to clear your name. I'll call my attorneys first thing in the morning. We are going to reopen the case."

"No way. I'm not going back to trial."

"It may never go to trial. It could be settled outside of court."

"How are we going to prove he did it?"

"Again, that's the lawyer's job. You have to trust me on this, Chase. You deserve to clear your name, and if you're telling me the truth, which I believe you are, then we can get this resolved and clear your record."

"You'd do that for me, bro?"

"Of course I would. You're my brother. Now, go make yourself at home. You can stay with me until this is resolved. You're not going anywhere."

~

After three hours in the ER, Emma was released with a boot on her foot and a diagnosis of a bad sprain. The entire time she was there, she had tried to get ahold of Chase, but his phone was powered off and it was going straight to voicemail.

She hadn't said more than two words to Aaron in the past three hours; she was still upset that he would do something so careless that could damage not only Chase's reputation but her own as well. As soon as she got out of his car, it would be the last time—she would be done with Aaron Reynolds once and for all.

Pulling into the driveway, her heart dropped to her stomach. The first thing she noticed was that Chase's motorcycle was gone, and no lights appeared to be on inside the guesthouse. She hoped that just meant he was at Ripples blowing off some steam. Surely, he hadn't left her. He'd made her a promise that he'd never leave her again. She wasn't pleased about this lie or his conviction, but she was willing to hear him out. She wanted to know his side of the story, and she wanted an explanation for why he had hid this from her.

"Look, Emma," Aaron started as he pulled into the driveway and put the car in park. "I'm sorry about the way—"

"Don't you dare," she cut him off through gritted teeth and opened her door to get out before turning to face him. "You could've come to me with this information. Instead, you decided to publicly humiliate not only Chase but myself as well. Now, not only can I not open my B&B, but this might have an impact on NovelTea as well. You singlehandedly set out to ruin my business and my reputation, so there is nothing you could say to me to ever make me trust you again." She managed to pull herself out of the car and slammed the door. She made her way around the car and toward the front door of Hemlock House as fast as she could on one good foot and a crutch.

"I'm not going to tell the committee about this, Emma," he called out the car window to her. "I never intended to."

She turned around to give him one final piece of her mind. "What difference does it make? Don't you think the entire town already knows by the scene you caused tonight?"

She made her way inside and slammed the front door before making her way to the parlor to collapse onto the couch in a fit of tears, Zeke loyally by her side trying to lick away the sadness.

Emma must have cried herself to sleep, because the next morning she awoke to find herself still on the couch. The first thing she did was make her way over to the side window to see if Chase's motorcycle had returned.

Her heart plummeted.

No sign of Chase. That meant he didn't come home last night. A series of terrible thoughts began racing through her mind. She had to get out to the guesthouse and see if he was back there. Maybe he'd had too much to drink and left his bike at Ripples.

She grabbed her crutch and made her way out the back door and across the lawn to the guesthouse. Taking a deep breath before twisting the knob, she gave the door a hard push with her hip.

When it swung open, nothing could have prepared her for what greeted her.

The guesthouse was empty. Lonely hangers hung in the closet. A ball of sheets in the middle of the bed. No duffel bag, no toiletries—no sign of Chase anywhere.

Emma sat down on the bed and clutched his pillow. His scent still lingering on it caused the tears to flow all over again. How could he leave her? Sure, she was upset, but that's only because he had lied to her. She never thought he would really leave. He had made her a promise that he'd never leave her again. He'd said he loved her, and she believed him. Had he lied about that, too?

The hollowness in Emma's heart caused a pain that took her back to the summer she was eighteen when he'd left her the first time. Only this time, it hurt far worse; because this time, she had fallen head over heels in love with him.

Emma sat on his bed, crying for what seemed like an eternity, until she realized she was late getting to NovelTea.

She went inside and took a hot shower in an attempt to wash away the pain. By the time the shower had ended, she'd made a pact with herself that she would put Chase out of her mind and get back to her everyday life. He was likely already out of the state by now, and there was no use mourning the loss of a relationship with someone who didn't truly love her.

Because if he loved her, he never would have left her. He would have at least said goodbye, and he hadn't even done that.

CHAPTER 16

"What in the world happened?" Rose asked, rushing out from around the counter to hold the door to NovelTea open for Emma, staring at the boot on Emma's foot with concern on her face.

"Long story," Emma said somberly. She looked around and noticed there wasn't a single person inside NovelTea besides Rose, and for once, she was grateful for it. She didn't know if she could put on a happy face for customers today.

"Uh-oh. What's going on?" Rose asked, a look of confusion in her eyes.

"So much has happened that I don't even know where to begin. I don't want to talk about it, actually." Emma made her way behind the counter before Rose came up and wrapped her in a hug. At the feeling of Rose's embrace, Emma started crying. It was times like those that she really missed her mother, and Rose always had a way of comforting her.

"Is it Chase?" Rose asked softly next to Emma's ear, still holding her tightly.

"Chase is gone, Rose," she finally said.

Rose pulled back and looked at her. "What do you mean?"

"There was a big to-do at the yacht club last night. Aaron came in and made quite a scene. He revealed details of Chase's past—things he had kept from me and lied about. Anyway, Chase ran out, I assumed because he was humiliated. His father had said some pretty harsh things to him."

"What did he have to say for himself?"

"That's the thing. I haven't talked to him. I hurt my ankle going after him and ended up in the ER for three hours. By the time I got home, he was gone. No note, no nothing."

"Have you tried calling him?"

"Straight to voicemail. He has his phone powered off."

"I'm sure he hasn't gone far. You two are set to open the B&B. I'm sure he will come to his senses. He's probably just embarrassed."

"No, you don't understand. There's no B&B after what Aaron did. As a matter of fact, I'm calling Arbor Shores Realty this morning. I'm listing Hemlock House; I'm putting it up for sale."

"What? Emma, don't make any rash decisions. Take some time and let your emotions settle."

"No, it's time. I don't need that big ole house for just me and Zeke. Plus, everywhere I turn is a constant reminder of the B&B and my future with Chase that is never going to happen. If you don't mind, I'd like to go sit in the office and call the realtor."

"If that's what you want to do. But I'd at least wait until you talk to him first."

"No, Rose. He's gone. Trust me, he left me once before and I didn't hear from him for eight years. Why would this time be any different?"

Emma hobbled back to the office on her crutch and shut

the door behind her. She pulled the small business directory out of her desk drawer and called the town's best realtor. She set a listing appointment for that afternoon.

There was no turning back now. She would get Hemlock House on the market and get herself a smaller house or an apartment. She just wanted out of the house and away from all the lost dreams that went with it as quickly as possible.

Emma made her way back up front to find there was only one regular at the counter having his morning coffee.

"Why don't you go on home, Emma. I can handle this myself today," Rose told her. Emma never missed a day of work, but something about Rose's offer sounded enticing. Her foot was throbbing and so was her heart. She could use a day on the couch feeling sorry for herself before the realtor showed up in a few hours.

"Thanks, Rose. I think I'll take you up on that."

The sun shining through the floor-to-ceiling window in Hunter's guest room was blinding. Chase woke up with no sense of purpose or anything to do with himself. He put a pillow over his head to block the invasive light. No reason to get out of bed today.

"Are you going to sleep all day?" he heard Hunter ask through a crack in the door.

Chase pulled the pillow off his head and looked at his brother. "What's the point of getting up?"

"Get a shower, and meet me downstairs. I have news," Hunter told him before closing the door.

Chase made his way to the en suite bathroom and turned on the shower. He wasn't moving quickly, and the ache behind his eyes dulled in comparison to the stabbing pain inside his chest every time he thought about Emma or replayed the events of the night before in his mind.

Twenty minutes later, he made his way downstairs to find his brother drinking a cup of coffee, reading the newspaper. "There you are, finally," Hunter said as Chase entered the kitchen. Hunter poured a cup of coffee and slid it to him across the white marble counter.

"What's the news?" Chase asked dryly. "He couldn't imagine anything his brother could say would lighten his mood.

"I spoke with my attorneys this morning. Conference call. They feel confident they can get this resolved for you. They are going to file a motion to reopen the case. They just need all the details from you, so you'll need to call them. Here's the number." Chase slid a business card across the counter.

"Seriously?" Chase picked up the card and inspected it.

"It may take some time, but they are going to get this off your record," Hunter told him, taking a sip from his cup.

"I don't know, Hunter. This person is a famous actor now. He probably has the best attorneys."

Hunter made his way around the island and placed a hand on Chase's shoulder. "Chase, you're a Knox. *We* have the best attorneys. If anyone can get this done, it's us."

"I don't know if I can really call myself a Knox. Dad disowned me last night."

"You'll always be a Knox. Don't worry about Dad. I'll explain what's going on to him. He'll come around. You know how his temper is. Sometimes he says things he doesn't mean."

"Well, after the things he said to me, I don't know if I care all that much *if* he comes around."

"I get that." Hunter poured out the rest of his coffee, rinsed the cup and put it in the dishwasher before turning to add, "I have to get going. Call the attorneys so they can get started."

"Hey, Hunter," Chase called out to him as his brother made his way toward the front door.

"Yeah?"

"Thank you for all you're doing for me. I appreciate it." Chase offered him the best smile he could muster up, given the circumstances.

"Of course. You're my brother. Everything is going to work out. Now, go get your girl back, man. Emma Woods is not the type of girl you let slip away." Hunter closed the front door and disappeared, leaving Chase alone in the house to contemplate those words.

The listing appointment went well, and to Emma's delight, the realtor thought she could get even more for the house than Emma had anticipated. Apparently, Chase fixing up the house had increased the value more than she'd expected. Since she owned Hemlock House outright, that meant she'd have a nice nest egg after the sale.

Emma stared out the front window and watched the realtor install the For Sale sign in the front yard. *Bittersweet.* On one hand she was ready to get out of this house and the memories that came with it, but she was also a bit disappointed that she had failed her parents. What would they think of her selling Hemlock House? This was their pride and joy, and she had always thought she'd own it forever as a way to keep their memory close. But now, it was just too much, and without earning an income from it, the best thing to do was to sell it to someone who could reopen it and make it as great as it once had been.

Emma took one final look at the For Sale sign and made her way back to the couch where she'd decided she'd spend the rest of the afternoon. Every so often, she checked her phone just to see if there was any chance Chase had called.

Nothing.

No texts, no calls, no voicemails. The hollowness left inside her chest was hard to ignore, but she resolved to stop dwelling on it, and at some point, she managed to doze off.

Chase called the attorneys like Hunter advised. His brother had been right; they sounded hopeful. They were reopening the case, and then going to work to prove his innocence. It was just going to take some time.

Hunter's final words before he left the house kept ringing in Chase's head. *Go get your girl back.* While Chase was certain Emma didn't want anything to do with him, he at least wanted the opportunity to tell her his side of the story. If she were willing to listen, that is.

He took the corners on Pine Ridge Way at top speed. Surely, Emma was at NovelTea, so he'd go straight there. Maybe she would agree to sit at a table and hear him out. He'd ruined any chance of a relationship. But if anything, maybe they could find a way to salvage their friendship again someday.

On his way to NovelTea, he had to pass Hemlock House. What was that in the yard? As he drew closer, it became undeniable. A punch to the gut nearly knocked him off his bike when he read the words: for sale.

He pulled his motorcycle to a stop in front of the house and stared at the sign in disbelief. Why was the house for sale? And how did that happen so quickly? He decided to get off his bike and go inside to see Zeke one last time. He owed it to that dog, and he missed him already. Of course, the front door would be unlocked since he never had been able to get Emma into the habit of locking it.

Making his way inside, he was greeted by Zeke at the front door. "Hey, boy," he said to him, leaning down to give him a good ear scratch and the apology that Zeke deserved.

Emma heard the front door open, and it woke her. Still lying on the couch in the parlor, she could hear Chase's voice. Relief surged through her and she exhaled for what felt like the first time all day. Chase was here? That meant he hadn't left, after all. She stayed quiet for a moment since he couldn't see her on the couch, and she wanted to hear what he was saying to Zeke.

"I'm sorry I left you the way I did, buddy. It's just that your momma is mad at me. I kept a secret from her, but that's only because I didn't think she'd love me if she knew the truth. You see, I didn't think I was good enough for her, and I didn't want her to think any less of me. Anyway, lesson learned because now I've lost her *and* you. She's probably going to fall in love with that Aaron fellow. I don't blame her though. He's better for her than I am. I just hope he's good to you. You'll tell me if he isn't, right boy?"

Emma inched her way quietly toward the foyer, listening to Chase's words to Zeke each step of the way.

"Anyway, I just wanted to tell you I'm sorry. Hopefully,

someday your momma will forgive me and she'll let me come by and see you sometime."

"I think that would probably be okay," Emma said, making her appearance in the foyer.

Chase stood up, wide-eyed, a look of shock and surprise splattered across his face. "Emma, I didn't know you were here. I figured you'd be at NovelTea." His gaze quickly fell to the boot on her foot. "What happened?"

"I was running after you last night, and I fell."

"So that's why you didn't come home?"

"Oh, I came home, just after spending hours in the ER. But by the time I got here, you were gone." She leaned against the doorframe to the foyer and looked down at the floor. "I figured you'd be far from Arbor Shores by now."

"When you didn't come home, I figured you were with Aaron," he admitted, shoving his hands into his pockets.

"Well, I *was* with Aaron, but only because I didn't have a choice. I couldn't drive so he took me to the ER."

"I'm sorry you hurt yourself on account of me." He took a step toward her.

"It's not your fault." Seeing Chase standing there, she wanted to throw her arms around him and tell him how happy she was that he hadn't left. She wanted to know where he'd been and why his stuff was gone. She wanted to ask why he'd lied to her and kept a secret from her. So many questions swirled in her mind; so many questions that she didn't even know where to begin.

"Em," Chase started before she could get a chance to say anything. "I just want you to know, I'm sorry I lied to you. It's the only lie I've ever told, and it was only because I didn't think you'd love me if you knew the truth. I didn't feel worthy of you, and I know that's no excuse, but it's the truth. I planned to tell you before we signed the papers. I promise I would have."

A long painful silence fell between them as she considered his apology. "I understand," she finally managed to get out.

"You do?"

"Yeah." She looked up at him. "I can understand not wanting to come home and tell everyone you'd been in jail, although you know you could have told me. I'd never think less of you. The only thing I don't understand is why you stole. Grand theft, Chase?"

"I was wrongfully accused, and I know that sounds like a lie and you have absolutely no reason to believe me, but I'm telling you the truth. Hunter's attorneys are reopening the case. They are already working to get it resolved and cleared from my record."

"That's great, Chase. I'm happy for you."

"Does that mean you believe me?" he asked.

Did she believe him? As much as she wanted to, part of her didn't trust his words completely. She had just found out he'd lied to her, and it was going to take some time for her to trust him again.

"Honestly, I don't know what to believe anymore, but I hope for your sake that's the truth."

"It is."

"So, you've been at Hunter's then?"

"Yeah. I'm staying there for now."

"I thought you left town."

"I was going to. I stopped there on my way out and told Hunter what happened. He insisted I stay and clear my name."

"So, that's why you stuck around? You did, actually, intend to leave?" She swallowed hard to try to dissolve the emotion that was bubbling to the surface.

"I thought that's what you wanted. I thought you had stayed with Aaron."

"Why would I want that, Chase? What I wanted was an explanation. What I wanted was my boyfriend to tell me the truth. What I wanted was for you to be here when I came home. What I wanted was—"

Chase took a step toward her. "Em, I wanted to give all that to you. I still do."

"You do?" She looked up at him, her eyes moist with tears threatening to spill. He was moving toward her, and the closer he got, the harder it was for her to stay mad at him. She just wanted him to wrap his arms around her and hold her. She longed for his embrace.

As if he were reading her mind, he slowly took her crutch out from under her arm and leaned it against the wall, eyes locked, holding her gaze. He took a final step closer, until no space remained between their bodies. He looked down at her and wrapped his strong arms around her waist and pulled her tightly into him. "Em, I love you. I never meant to hurt you. I understand if you don't want to be with me because of my past, but I hope someday you can find it in your heart to forgive me. You're my best friend, and I don't want to lose you."

She rested her hands on his shoulders and looked into his eyes. "What kind of woman would I be if I didn't want to be with you over a mistake you made in your past? Of course I want to be with you." The words came out on their own, before she had a chance to contemplate them, but she meant them. She'd never been so relieved to see Chase in her foyer, and she never wanted to lose him again.

"You do?"

"Yes. I love you, Chase," she whispered.

He swooped down and took her mouth in his, kissing her with a passion more intense than anything she had yet to feel from him. His hands moved from her waist to the sides of her face. She latched her fingers behind his neck, pulling him in, taking the kiss deeper. The kiss seemed to last forever, so long that Zeke began snoring at their feet.

When they finally broke apart, Chase asked, "Hey, what's with the For Sale sign in the front yard?"

"I was going to sell Hemlock House. I didn't want to be here without you," she whispered.

"Can you take if off the market?"

Emma smiled. "I'll call the realtor."

*T*he grand opening of Hemlock House was a huge success. Even Carter and Valerie showed up to support Emma and Chase, along with the rest of the crew and most of the residents of Arbor Shores.

It took six long months, but the lawyers had managed to clear Chase's name. Turns out, Hunter's attorneys were every bit as good as he had said, and they were able to get a confession from the young actor. The conviction was removed from Chase's record, and while he would never get the time back he had served, he was just thankful to not only have a clean record, but also to have the support of his family, friends, and the entire community—sans Aaron Reynolds who, of course, was not invited.

He may never be close to his father after the things Carter had said to Chase that night at the yacht club, but at least he'd shown up to offer his support, and that meant something.

Emma and Chase cut the ribbon out front as the reporter from the *Arbor Shores Beacon* snapped photos for the local paper, and everyone cheered at the official opening of the

B&B. The party moved inside where Chase and Emma had hors d'oeuvres and cocktails for their guests, and everyone took turns taking a tour of the massive Victorian home that would be welcoming guests, effective immediately.

Chase and Emma moved back outside for a moment to admire Hemlock House and take it all in. They embraced in the front yard, and then Chase turned and got down on his knee, taking Emma's left hand in his. A nervous excitement jolted through him as he looked up at her in anticipation.

"Emma Woods, you're my best friend, my companion, my business partner, my everything. I can't imagine spending a single day of my life without you in it. Let's grow old in Hemlock House together, just like your parents had planned. Let's live out their love story that got cut short and taken from them far too early. Would you make me the happiest man alive and be my wife? Will you be Mrs. Emma Knox?"

Emma quickly nodded her head yes, tears streaming down her face, her smile as wide as the sun. Chase slipped an engagement ring on her finger and rose to his feet, wrapping her in his arms, and sealing their engagement with a kiss as everyone came out and cheered from the front porch.

Everything had come full circle, and Emma and Chase were not only partners in business, but partners in life.

Chase Knox finally had a place to call home.

Want more of Arbor Shores? Check out: *Christmas Getaway for Two: Christmas in Arbor Shores Book One.*

ABOUT THE AUTHOR

Nomi Summers is a clean contemporary romance author with a flair for taming bad boy heroes readers swoon over.

When she's not dreaming up her next small town romance, you'll find her at the beach devouring the latest new release on her Kindle. Her other guilty pleasures include getting lost in mindless reality TV and spending far too much time talking to her dogs, as she's convinced they understand every other word!

Nomi's living her own "happily ever after" with her loving husband and their two fur babies in Tampa Bay, Florida. However, a piece of her heart will always belong in Michigan where she's originally from—the inspiration behind the settings in her novels.